COMMERCIAL ROAD:
SHORT STORIES

BY

RAPHAEL AGBOWU D'CRUZ

Copyright

Copyright © 2023 Raphael Agbowu D'Cruz

All rights reserved.

First paperback edition. July 2023

ISBN: 9798396692558

Book cover design by Ezekiel Akinnewu.

For all my family, friends, and dedicated to my late grandparents:

Jill D'Cruz, whose infectious love and kindness truly knew no bounds.

Trevlyn D'Cruz, whose knowledge was only ever outweighed by his charm.

Diana Durban, and her everlasting wisdom. She always loved a story.

To auntie Tina. Life of the party.

CONTENTS

Title Page

Copyright

Dedication

Contents

Sun or Death?

Eden's Song

Commercial Road

About the Author

SUN OR DEATH?

'Single or double?'

Asks the hottest bartender, for ten square miles. Perhaps twenty. I know the ends, and all it has to offer. This girl here, one of a kind. Wavy hair, matching gold hoops. She may be wearing the same clothes as the rest of them but this uniform, bland as shit, fails to displace her aura for anonymity. Don't even get me started on her eyes, green with a hint of...

'A single it is, then.'

I should stop. With my shades on, I look around and head bop to the mashup of Kojo and Hus, albeit controversial, not that anyone here cares anymore. Nines and Biz, Chip and Bugzy, this dance floor thrives off of beef. Yet, all I'm actually doing, is thinking of a line whilst watching her, back turned, as she pours up my two drinks.

Single. Double.

I am single, that's the lead in, but what's the punchline? I need some quick wit. Now the Wray's been poured up, she's reaching for the soda gun, until she remembers, I explicitly asked for apple. Reaching below to retrieve the juice, she looks up at me briefly, and I turn away. Even my shades leave me defenceless against her power, fam.

The drinks are poured and presented. I pretend to notice it late, nodding to a guy afar, who's not even there.

'Ok, 14.50, please. Just tap here.'

I tap in. This is it.

'Safe. Next time, maybe me and you can double it up,' I say, tilting my shades as I grab the rum and apple mixers. But as soon as I do so, I come to notice, she's already turned away to serve the next customer. So now I'm left there, lingering, and even more embarrassed.

It's way too hot up here, I think to myself, with a careful eye on the drinks as I carefully lay them down to remove my jumper. A shame because it's so fresh, cost a bag along with the Forces on the fifth floor of Selfridges. But I'm sweating out here, and the drip ain't worth it.

'You're tapped, man,' says Jordan upon my arrival, 'coming like Columbus every time you hit the bar.'

He snatches his drink. 'Not every day sightseeing.'

'At least I ain't colonising half the bar on my way back, that shit works in reverse nowadays.' At last, a slice of wit I can dish out and be proud of, accompanied by my nod, to gesture the heaving dance floor facing our table.

My slim smile fades when an unapologetically loud group of gin and tonic girls begin to scream Skepta lyrics. Each of them rapping a verse whilst the rest of the rooftop observes from each corner, half bopping their heads, the other half watching their asses. I look back to Jordan, spitting Blacklisted like it's gospel.

'Same shit different day! Same shit different day!'

I turn my attention to the Prosecco-sipping DJ, his signet pinkie ring raised to the sky, doing the same.

'What's up with you today, Kyle?'

We're on a rooftop bar, one that used to be lowkey. Then it got bought, sold and flipped again, and now it's owned by, of all companies, Wray and Nephew. We're surrounded by others, all dancing, slurring words, arms around each other, and ultimately, soaking up the sun. It's four PM, bank holiday Monday, August. Them ones.

So, nothing should be wrong with me. 'Heatstroke.'

My quick response, a legitimate term that surely demands no further explanation, does nothing for Jordan.

'Kyle, we run too deep for you to lie to me. If you want to move to them lot, or anyone else here, I got you. Wingman ting, it's a minor.'

I follow Jordan's gaze to another group of girls, up on the tables, twerking to afro-beat mixes.

He smirks at the sight of them. 'Just 'cos I'm signed now, don't mean I've got to stop bagging. Even if it's an assist.'

I sip my drink. 'You know that ain't my type.'

That one gets a laugh, unintentional, but I'll take it, and Jordan eyes me when downing his drink. He gives me that look, the one he always flashes, whether in the depths of a rave, or around the table at my Mum's flat. That sure look of disapproval.

'Anyway, today we're celebrating, bro. I'm with you, forget the noise.' Jordan waves over to a waitress, who presents a shot tray to our messy table. He taps his card and takes the last two. As much as overproof does terrify me, due to past experiences, there's still nothing like a clean shot of white rum. I take mine in hand.

Jordan raises his. 'Toast me up, I just got the news. Today, my son's being born.'

Clink. The shots spill onto each other as we bash them together and gulp in sync. That's when the news hits me, even harder to swallow. Trust him to be waved with me when she's in labour.

I cough up half my shot and, hands to my chest, run straight for the nearest bathroom. Jordan laughs me off as I do so. I weave my way through the bar, and into the nearest cubicle, to begin throwing up everything I've got left in me. Even the guy in the adjacent cubicle bangs the wall, showing concern, before also laughing at my own expense. But not me, especially when I clock the colour of my vomit, which is red. I swear, this heat's killing me.

I kick down my cubicle and waddle through this narrow mess of a bathroom, my vision a blur. With my ears ringing from the hand dryer, I know something's off. As if the constant feelings of dread, in any given social situation, doesn't do me enough damage.

When I push open the door, I almost collapse with it, but Jordan catches me.

'Come, down some water and sit in the shade. You're good.' Jordan's unfazed by the attention his fireman's lift demands, as he parades me through the rooftop bar.

I'm the opposite, drowning in a pool of shame, plus a more literal puddle of vomit streaming down my new shirt. Nothing left to lose, until the embarrassment skyrockets once we pass the bar, and I catch the stare of that same flawless bartender, giggling in my direction.

Once Jordan slams me back into my seat, that same waitress with the shot tray arrives, this time with water.

Jordan hands me the jug with a wink, then looks back to her. 'This what your presence does to people then, B?'

Jordan flirtatiously signals for the waitress to swoop down, so he can whisper into her ear. Even back in school, this guy knew no bounds. Jordan would employ the exact same tactic with the taller year-elevens from our first day in uniform. Maybe, well maybe is a bit of a stretch, for definite, this is the reason why I eventually latched onto him. So, what was in it for him, in this up and down, at times stressful, occurrence we like to call brotherhood?

Well, other than reminding him of the power of his slick, cool, confident outlook on life, I listened. To this day, I listened whenever he wants to complain about the perils of a carb-cutting meal plan for the sake of gains, or whenever his manager dropped him since he would always chat back. Throughout all, I listened.

I look to him now, proudly taking the digits from this hostess, all the while, his girl's somewhere across the maze of South London, about to give birth, wondering where her man is. But don't even get me started on Jade.

Still, Jordan's my best friend, always has been, and always will be. The two of us do everything together. He's been there for me throughout all, especially recently, ever since Vanessa left. He picked me back up, like a true brother, and every time, he did it with ease.

'I'm not going to blame you Kyle, but you got to know how to step in the bank holiday heat.'

Says the man who practically dressed me for today. Each message I would send to him, asking about a time and place for our next link up, and he would hit me back, almost exclusively about drip.

Trust me cuz, on Monday, wear the Forces.

Those Forces now painted red with vomit, and my white t-shirt, now off-white, from the rum.

Sometimes I've got to get out of my own head, even if it is better to live inside it, and embrace the summertime. Too many days I avoided stepping out, everyone belling my phone and to be fair, I've simply ran out of excuses.

Oddly enough, the second I do manage to feel better and, on the mend, someone at the adjacent table throws up all over the floor. I can only imagine working here, cleaning up the relentless storm of hipsters, trappers, and city workers alike. I sneak a peek at their vomit. Blood.

'The Wray's got you all moving mad. That ain't me,' laughs Jordan.

Throw it back to last Friday, when he's blackout drunk, the club's closed, and it was me who walked him home, when all his teammates cut. Not that he thanked me for it, or ever will do. But laughing at his jokes is quicker than an interrogation about how moody I am all the time, despite the fact that my jokes fly way over his head.

'We both know deep down you got that white girl tolerance. Add it to your bio,' I joke, proudly.

Jordan responds with a scolding look, from head to toe, ready to hit back until his phone violently vibrates. Eventually, he picks it up and shields the muffled voice.

'Come on, you know I'm there. I'm on my way.'

Jade. Maybe I should say something, even shake the man until he realises the magnitude of his situation. If it were up to Jordan, he'd probably skip the entire birth, plus each following year, in order to reach the good part, where the kid can kick ball and sign for Chelsea U-11's.

Now, that ain't me. 'Let's go, Jordan, she needs you.' Straight over his head, again. Anything I say.

After Jordan slides his chair out and straightens his t-shirt creases, he extends his phone towards me. 'Golden hour, Kyle. Snap me?'

We waltz past the dance floor to the beat of RnB slow jams, and make it to the front, to reach the sweet spot and soak up the picturesque skyline. London, it really is like no other, if only for six days a year. Backs are turned, phone cameras flash, and cue the peace and gang signs, at this bar's infamous spot. Most are swapping phones, politely asking strangers to snap them and their entire crew, but I'm stuck here taking photos of Jordan's numerous Zoolander poses. He vocally directs me, it's embarrassing. Jordan quickly senses that my attention is fixed on the mesmerising sun right behind him, instead.

'Quick,' he asserts, posing for the money shot. I take multiples, and Jordan checks them over, then approves with a slight nod. The sun is setting fast, and by now, whoever hasn't got their shots, will probably have to return again for the same thing, tomorrow.

Now, we're all just left gazing up at it. The slow jams leave my peripheral, and I can't stop staring. To my right, then to my left, I look around to see it's the same for all the others. The sun sits unbelievably close to us, a bright beaming red, and jaws are dropping at the sheer sight of it. The heat seems to match this intensity, the lower it falls the hotter it feels, and it's almost unbearable. I feel a hand on my shoulder, pulling, tugging me, but I ignore it. That hand shifts to a firm shove, and as soon as I'm forced to turn away, I realise that everyone else is long gone. In this moment, I'm so hot, so dizzy, my hands to my knees. I forget where I am, who I am, or who I was even with.

I backtrack to observe the other customers, all gathered in front of me. They're intently looking down at something, and I'd bet my money on it being some girl whining on another man. Yet, this time, for a first, I might even retract that bet. For, when I finally swivel away from the glistening sun, surely closer to us than ever, casting a blood-red glow shadow onto the ground, I nearly jump out of my skin. Jordan eyes me, with a deafening stare.

There's been a murder on the dance floor.

I throw up at the sight of it, but I'm not the only one. At the centre of the dance floor, directly beneath the rooftop's glass exterior, lies a body. Others surround it. It's hard to tell what went down, but equally as alarming, is the huge cluster of people surrounding the body, throwing up. It's as if an invisible wave has passed through us all, one by one. The worrying thought is, they're spewing blood, so whatever this is, I must have it too. I'm also doomed.

'They need to shut this spot down. Must be in the water, the system. I don't know, but we better cut.' Jordan's remark is accompanied by a new casualty. By the second, partygoers faint and bite the dust, and my anxiety spikes to record levels. Actually, that's a lie. It's at a record-breaking rate when I spot a call, from Jade. I stare down my ringing phone.

Jordan catches on and I attempt to casually pick up the phone, to ask Jade if she's good. Of course she's not, in the midst of giving birth on the hottest day of the decade. I really do suck at one-liners.

'Who's belling you?' asks Jordan, suspiciously.

I dodge his question with another glance around, to see that the rooftop has descended into full blown chaos. I decide that I cannot keep this one from him, the stakes are too high.

'We need to go, get to Jade, before this madness means we can't holler a ride.' My instruction is firm. Another buzz strikes my knee, as Jade texts again.

NOW, K.

I lift wipe my forehead and shove Jordan towards the exit, clogged with people as panic, propelled by the viciously rising heat, sweeps through us all.

I remove my shades and sneak in another long look up at the sun. There's a different energy to it now, simultaneously drawing you in then burning you with regret, for simply glancing up at it.

Jordan drags me through the crowd and fights his way through with impeccable timing, since the glass doors behind us collapse as soon as we pass through them, with an earth shattering effect.

I spot a shard of glass lodged deep into my forearm. Any wincing pain surpasses, as I lock onto the sun, now twice as close to us since I last checked.

Then comes a violent roar from the sky above, the type of loud bang we only associate with winter weather. Our collective fear skyrockets, startled to the core when the corridor is suddenly rumbled by a thunder strike and earthquake alike. That was Mother Nature herself, I'm thoroughly convinced, rumbling the floorboards all the way up towards the singular exit, a spiral staircase which would never have seemed sturdy enough to fit this manic crowd, even on an ordinary day. But no bar should have to account for a literal stampede of its customers.

Once we reach the bottom of the staircase, Jordan reaches for his phone and gets swiping. I glimpse a fast taxi app, the screen buffering, but before it fully loads, his phone is sent flying backwards. It's impossible to spot the culprit within this apocalyptic flood of Londoners. I've never seen so much action take place inside a jazz bar. Tables and chairs are dispersed, each customer fighting to forge their own paths, through to the outside. Screams form the newest anthems inside, so we no longer require a DJ and trap tunes to fill the void within.

Speaking of, I spot the DJ dash behind the bar to raid the fridge for Prosecco, then sneak off through the back.

'This way,' I whisper. I grab Jordan, to stop him from furiously rummaging around for his phone, and we run.

There's a long millisecond between our dive over the bar, where we mutually acknowledge the fact, that we were made for this kind of adventure. In fact, we've subconsciously been waiting for it our whole, entire lives. Too many nights at mine re-watching *Enter the Dragon*, or anything Bruce Lee. Our excitement rises tenfold when the DJ meets us on the other side of the bar, shielding himself with a broom, and Jordan ducks to hit him with a brutal upper cut. We then spud one another, I even laugh.

Then we're back at it. A short interval to help us forget the scale of this odd nightmare, unfolding before our very own eyes. Jordan takes lead and rushes past the bar into the keg room, and before he slams the door shut behind us, I sneak a glance at the chaos unfolding out front. Half the tide turns our way, to spot the open door. Frenzied faces hop over the bar to head in our direction. A full on horde.

We rush into the backdoor and Jordan kicks down the second, leading into the staff room. That's when I stop, because inside, curled up in a ball, is her. That bartender. Terrified, she stares up at us.

'Where's the door!' yells Jordan. Definitely not helping this scenario whatsoever. I help her up with a forced smile of reassurance. She instinctively takes my hand, pointing right with the other, to a fire exit.

At last, we are faced with a stairwell that leads to the outside. We race down it as a trio, skipping every other stair as we practically skip the whole set. Upon our first step outside, we're hit with a wave of heat unlike any other I'm yet to experience in this city. If only I knew the Miami heat was willing to visit us, as I would have saved myself all the racks spent to fly out. Of course, that holiday was Jordan's idea, he simply laughed when I suggested Budapest. Instead, we travelled halfway across the planet, to shed our savings on VIP tables, which were inevitably filled with all the other British non-VIP's.

Although, this heat isn't the good kind, and I'm more than worried. Even worse, is the fact that the sun is now angled incredibly low, as if it's speaking directly to me. I'm no scientist, but with my proud triple-science GSCE's, I can tell, it really isn't in a good mood. In fact, another short lived stare up at it tells me it's mad, with some good reason to be. Humans, that shit's on all of us.

Eventually, the crowd catches up to us, which isn't a good sign at all. We share a brief stare back at them, tripping over each other while the girls, once chauffeured by the horny men around them, are now being trampled on by the very same people. The mandem take precedence, swiping hipsters away with every move, to reach the front of the horde, without any remorse.

Despite avoiding the rush, we involuntarily take its lead, irritated by the fact that we are being pursued by the very same lot we need to get away from, to guarantee our safety. Left with no other option than to face the heat, we advance past the shady haven of the smoking area situated out front.

That's when I feel it. A burn like no other, seeping deep into my skin by the millisecond. I look to my glass-shattered arm, it's now sizzling. As if the tan that requires a month in Ibiza, or half a day in a tanning bed to achieve, is instant, like a time lapse.

'Come.' The bartender's strict order is enough to revert our attention back to the matter at hand here.

We sprint forwards. Jordan runs from behind, and as he always does so, overtakes me with ease. We follow the bartender into an alleyway to finally find some shade. Panting, sizzling, and shocked by the steam emitting from our trio of arms and legs, we look up.

'Don't,' says the bartender. I take one last look.

The bartender soon announces her name to Jordan. Daniella, I hear her say it to him, but when watching them both speak, with panic so infused in every line, I begin to tune out. I'm losing my senses.

'I said swing your phone, Kyle,' utters Jordan, 'focus.'

'You know how to get here, without all the heat?' Jordan's question is met with a shrug from Daniella, who screw-faces the phone and pinches the screen, a task in itself with her lilac acrylic nails, to grasp the location. Jade's location. Our end goal.

They look clueless, it's time for me to step in. 'Jade should've been at Kings, but they couldn't get to her in time. She's still at her mum's place. Big enough to have a baby in, and then some, init?'

Jordan scolds me for the insight, bitter at the thought that I should know such a thing about her. 'Bless, we keep moving. I will be there for my son.'

I point left, not entirely sure if it's the correct route, but all the alleyways lead from Peckham to Dulwich soon enough. We're five minutes off, but I can't shake the thought that we're in for a challenge that requires the same endurance to journey to Mordor and back. If Jordan is to be our Frodo, then I've got to step up and really be on my Gandalf shit.

Speaking of old men and their long white beards, once we reach the end of the alleyway, we're soon obstructed. From out of nowhere, an old man creeps up on us from inside an industrial bin, popping the lid. I only relax when I spot a crazed look in his eye.

'Time to repent!'

I stop Jordan from one-banging him back into the bin. He fails to make this man flinch, and instead, he flashes a wide gap-tooth smile. I like him already.

The man continues, 'good deeds from now, my friends. My man up there, he's watching all you,' he stalks us down the alley. 'So, you got any change?'

Jordan can't bear to stall any longer. 'You best move, or I swear, I'll find you in hell, then you'll be missing that shit and piss-hole you just came from.'

The man bursts into hysterics, I sweep in to show him the phone. His stare meets mine, and scepticism clashes optimism. 'Know how to get here, fast?'

The man clears his throat, places an arm on me. 'Lucky, you've got six, seven minutes, according to science. See up there? The sun is dying, my friends. Dying for our redemption!'

I toss him my last twenty, not that I'll need it if that is the case. He uses it to blow his nose, enroute back to his bin. We rush to the end of the alleyway, but we all momentarily pause when we do reach it. The shade stops here.

Daniella points us towards the next alleyway, situated right across the road. Easy in normal circumstances, but inbetween, the empty road is painted red, haunted by the looming ghost of the sun, from up above. That's when Daniella gives in, tugs the straps of her bag, and lets out a long sigh. She winces at her own arm, when feeling her burns.

My eyes are on her bag. 'You got clothes in there?'

Daniella removes the bag and I unzip it to spot a two jumpers, a bucket hat, plus shades, and wipes. While rummaging through, I also retrieve a pack of condoms, awkward as I tuck the box back inside. 'We need to wrap up warm, but not that warm.'

If only I could rehearse or reverse these moments, for when they happen, I'm the one to forever regret them. Yet, Daniella's giggle is actually a slight relief.

'You heard the donny, we need to fucking step.' Jordan, understandably vexed and impatient, attempts to bulldoze into the road, only to return with a scorching burn. Cursing as he consoles his bicep, equally fascinated to see his AK47 tattoo, fully eradicated. He studies it closely, until I chuck over one of Daniella's jumpers, plus a bucket hat to wear.

'Trust me,' my tone drops between those two words, half believing it myself, that this may work.

We play dress up to protect our skin. Still half exposed, I head back towards the bin and pop open the scorching hot lid, to kindly ask the old man for some layers. But I stop myself short, stunned, as I'm met with the sight of his corpse. He's been skin fried.

Still, there's some clothes left on him, an entire wardrobe, in fact. The others join me, and I spot their same expressions of disgust as they realise, too. We rummage through, avoiding the remnants of Mr Old Man. I opt for an odd fit that includes a khaki trench coat with battered grey joggers, and lowkey, my blue cardigan seems to match Daniella's drip.

Urgency strikes again, and Jordan leads us forwards, into the deserted road. It's less intense, but a tough task, nonetheless. Cue the dehydration.

The twenty second sprint required to cross this vast and empty road seems to be the best we are able to achieve. Although, protecting our skin from the burns, wearing layers amidst the rising heat, of course, has its downsides. Once we reach the opposite end, rushing far into the alley and clinging to the walls for maximum shade, the three of us are depleted. I look to Daniella, clinging to a wall to consume the shade, as she sinks to the floor. Then I look to Jordan, licking his lips in futile fashion. It makes me want lick mine, but I spot my lips through his shades, they have almost completely peeled off.

No time for a pitstop. Jordan, without a word, stands back up to stride on and maintain our momentum. I follow, but as we scale the alleyway, I look back to see Daniella stand up ever so slowly, and collapse. I decide to do the right thing, and jog back towards her.

'I know we just met, but together we'll pull through, Daniella. Stay, and it's likely, you'll die.'

My last few words, the cold matter of fact, sugar coated and wrapped in plastic, seem to do the trick. Daniella, with her arm strapped to mine, drags her feet towards Jordan, who's impatiently jogging on the spot. You might call this a good deed if it really is judgement day. Beneath that lies my true thought; I desperately need someone to save me instead.

Luck arrives in the form of liquid. We stop for water. The moment we cross into Dulwich through a maze of backstreets, we spot a small, beaten down corner shop. This one's tucked below the ground floor beneath a towering estate, which provides just enough support to shield the building from the heat, thanks to the balcony above providing us with enough shade. Trust the local boss man to prove so crucial on a day like this. We need to hydrate, and I feel Jordan's eyes through the back of my head knowing that by we, I really just mean Daniella.

'Be quick,' hisses Jordan. I lack the energy to respond. He knows where we're headed, he's made that clear, and at this point, there is no getting to Jade if we don't see to the real priority at hand.

Survival.

God knows how many sudden deaths have occurred on this road alone in the last half an hour, whether burns or pure dehydration. God also knows how desperate I am for us to make it to safety and reach Jade's place, too. Trust me on that one.

Speaking of, as soon as we enter the shop my phone rings, and I decline it. I'm surprised it still even works, but 5G in the apocalypse is definitely the kind of thing I expected as a customer, despite paying a killing a month for the signal to cut whenever I'm scrolling socials on the train, my sofa, or anywhere else of use. Daniella rushes past me to a fridge by the counter, to grab and sink down whatever she can find. Just as she throws me an off-brand blue electrolyte drink, the kind I would never have chosen before this mess, I'm hit with a round of texts. I know from whom, before I even check: Jade, Jade, Jade.

Speak to me, K. BEFORE WE ALL FUCKING DIE.

That's just one of the many texts. I pocket the phone and grab some drinks to supply Jordan with.

'Hey,' says Daniella, squeezing the ends of a bottle, 'I'm not coming. I'm not going back out there. I just can't. You heard that guy, what's the point?'

I process it but my mind drifts to my vibrating pocket. 'We're so close. Once there, I'll make a plan.'

Those words just spill out of my mouth, I feel like I'm mostly trying to convince myself, but what else can I say? To admit defeat would be exactly what they all, well, what Jordan expects from me. This time, I'll be the one to find a way out, should it be my last act. Give up or show up, the truth that stands is, I'll probably die either way.

Further attempts of mine to persuade Daniella to believe in the goal of safety, as vaguely as I put it, are fruitless. It's as if I were a motivational speaker, keeping mental hostages by teasing the keys to success to sell stadium tickets. I even failed at that.

I lose the will to listen to my own speech, and end up standing there, guiltily sucking on an ice cube, also thinking of the perils of stepping back outside. The silence consumes this deserted corner shop, which must have been bustling with bank holiday beer sales this very same morning. Then Daniella, with an injured, dehydrated wobble, edges closer and much to my surprise, swoops in and kisses me. 'Good luck out there, Kyle.'

I couldn't convince her. Daniella's choice to stay, whether smart or not, is a fixed one. Time will tell.

'Trust the end of the world to be why you finally try and spit some game.' That, and every other spiteful comment from Jordan, fills my peripheral as we drag ourselves onwards. By this point, even the apocalypse seems to fade into the background. I feel sick, nauseous, my mouth so dry and my body so unbearably hot, I can't fight back. Dehydration has seeped right into my being and wrapped itself right around my subconscious. We're simply done for.

We've only made it ten metres away from our pit stop, each few steps forces us into shade to recharge. Still not far enough to shake the thought of Daniella.

'Risking it all for some random yat, a new low for you. Could've been there time ago.' Jordan leans against a wall, basking in the slim shadows, while I avoid his glare. The sun, it's now practically above my head, I can't help but think why we haven't melted like cheese strings. South London's a desert. Even if everyone is cowered in a bunker somewhere, I doubt we would have the energy left to find it.

The main paradox here is the absence of familiarity- obliterated trees and cars, the rest reduced to ashes- while this also just feels like any other day on the ends. Scaling local roads we know like the back of our hands, another routine roast from my best friend being the only thing to leave a true burn on me.

Today, I've finally heard enough.

'Shut the fuck up, J.' As if there were any real beating heart to penetrate, least not with words.

Jordan, depleted of energy himself, laughs back, his voiced hinged on mania. 'Don't lie to yourself. You've always had to hide behind me, scrape whatever seconds you can get, I'm cool with it. Now the world falls apart and you try to live a fantasy. But you ain't shit.'

My phone rings in my pocket. Jade's timing is quite something special. I slide my phone out and chuck it afar.

'That her? Pick it up, fam. The fuck you doing?' Jordan spits his curse and darts towards my shadow. I dodge it, he quickly counters, to grab my throat.

I'm swung like a ragdoll and pinned up against the wall like a UFC fight, and it feels just like old times. From kids playing WWE, to the real deal. The TV did warn us. Professor X versus Magneto, Obi-Wan versus Anakin. Any dynamic duo you can name, inevitably turns on each other to become fierce rivals. Just charge that one to the game.

Jordan grabs my phone and promptly, it rings. 'Jade? Near, baby. I'm close. I'm coming to get you,' he cuts his sentence to face me, both eyes bulging, 'the fuck you wanna speak to Kyle for? I'm here.'

Intuitively, my focus switches to something else. I spot the shop, Daniella's shop, erupting in flames.

So, I run. Not before I shove Jordan away with all my might and accelerate faster than Rashford back towards her. I look back to see Jordan, also sprinting, not to assist me like Rice or Saka would do, but to chase me down at full pelt instead. The tables have turned, and now it seems, we're playing for different countries, and I'm good with that. The adrenaline heightens my senses, I can just feel Jordan foaming from the mouth, spitting my name through a storm of explosive rage. I think he knows.

Not like this, I thought I would have had more time to tell him. I also thought I would have had more time for a lot of things, before this wild, greatly unprecedented day arrived. I know the truth surely would have been served to him with a piping hot side dish of heart break. That wound then salt-sprinkled with the crystals of shame. I know I would have done it better, all of this, if only I still had time.

A harrowing scream emits from inside the corner shop, a high-pitched piercing call, of death, which doesn't exactly resemble Daniella's pitch, either.

'Help ME,' the wailing loops as if on a scratched vinyl. The fifth time round, I pause at the shop door.

Adrenalines supposed to propel you into these kinds of situations, but of course knowing my luck, it fails to do so. Heart thumping, burning up, both from the sun in its terminal state, plus the roaring flames right in front, I simply stand there, helpless. Frozen against fire. Seconds drag and it soon becomes apparent, this fire is quite literally, alive.

Inside, a flailing man, set alight by the flames, darts back and forth, knocking over everything in his path. Then, as Jordan edges nearer, his pursuit is enough to kickstart my dive into the depths of hell, to save her. Daniella, the girl I hardly even know. Perhaps I was always destined to be Batman, or whatever low-budget equivalent it is that Peckham needs. Just a man, your bang average Kyle, jumping head-first into a flaming hot shop I grew up in, buying, but most of the time stealing, from. Probably to never make it out, but I guess I'll die trying. Jordan watches me, taking that leap of faith.

The figure inside shop is quite the embodiment of our times. A headless chicken let loose in the product aisles.

'HELP ME.'

Each time, his words are fuelling the fire, bumping hard into every other shelf, knocking Heinz bean tins, KitKat's, and Powerade's alike, to the floor. Then there is Daniella, cowered low under a counter, similar to how we first found her, earlier on today. She faces me, I face her through the holes in the blue cardigan that I'm using as a shield against the thick haze of smoke. I race over to Daniella until I'm instantaneously knocked sideways by this man. He lifts me up with a blazing hot hand.

Stunned, I look straight into his eyes, the only recognisable thing left, as he repeats himself to me, 'Help. hell...'

That failed attempt at his own infamous catchphrase is also his last. I watch as his lips disintegrate along with his skin, as his arms flop to the floor, melting into ash. This scratched record finally snaps, his soundtrack sticks and replays in my head. Hell. I couldn't have described it any better. Distracted, I slowly clock on to my own flaming arm.

Whoever designed this cardigan deserves an award. Mr. old man from the bins is also the G.O.A.T. for copping, stealing, trading, or buying it. Whatever means necessary. Either way, that man has already saved my life more times than I can count, and he definitely deserved way more than just a score. I deflect the fire by frantically stomping it out around me, to forge a path.

No highs without the lows, it's true today of all days. I'm left sick to my stomach with regret because the moment I triumphantly rush to come to Daniella's aid, is also the moment I realise I really did screw up. Big time. The fire, which is actually fuelled by my blue cardigan, has now spread behind us and engulfed the shop. I find Daniella at the heart of this mess, coughing up ferociously, then duck down, as the ceiling collapses in on the pair of us.

Luckily, the ceiling crash makes way for a small opening inside the shop walls, and I'm left with no other alternatives. With Daniella strapped to my back, I race towards the wall and shield her against the falling bricks, as well as the spontaneous uproar of flames we face with each step. To my surprise, when we finally do reach this hole in the wall, now at an arm's length, another arm strongly extends itself past the opening, to assist me as I weave us through it. It seems we do play for the same team. Jordan's divine timing crucially saves us both, and I sling Daniella over my shoulder for one last ditched effort as I take Jordan's hand and pull us to safety.

It doesn't stop there. The world outside has risen up in flames, now the shop fire has spread, to chase us down. We run faster than ever towards the furthest corner away from this hell pit. Along the way, I notice something terrifyingly odd about Jordan's sprint, and I spot his flesh-peeling skin. That momentous worry is quickly displaced by the urge to check on Daniella, as I pull her from over my shoulder onto the ground, to check on her pulse.

My own heart skips a beat, then another. I'm croaking my plea through a coughing fit as I rest my ear above her chest, but fail to hear anything. Every resuscitation technique my subconscious has ever archived from a life undeniably spent watching more films than the average man, a sure means of escape, now kicks into gear. I try to revive her. I'm then served a true, gut-punching reminder that this is no movie, I'm no hero, and she isn't magically due to wake up coughing, nor show any vital signs of life. Throughout the shock, deafening coughs, and surrounding fires, I try to force myself to realise this. I did all I could, but still, that just wasn't enough.

Daniella's death was neither graceful, nor justified. I messed up by leaving her and even now, as I stare down at her lifeless body, I realise that. Even worse is the fact that there's no time to mourn, grieve, reflect, or ensure any dignity for her fresh corpse. I can't even face the sun to direct my resentment at something, at someone, and in the name of survival, we are forced to leave her behind.

Back again, to just the two of us, but Jordan's sick. When you've known someone for this long, matters such as this really do go without saying. I can just sense it. Perhaps the death of the sun is spreading delusion with it but, regardless, between Jordan and I, a strange yet tangible type of telepathy has always existed, ever since day one.

It's came and gone throughout the years and fed off of our bond, but even on the days we don't speak, I feel his presence, more so his mood swings, or he feels mine. Whenever I sunk my day into internet wormholes to evade the outside world, I would always feel his footsteps, rocking up to my door to force me back out again before it even happens. Right now, that feeling is more powerful than ever.

We're so close now, just metres away from Jade, but I fear he won't make it.

'Wait up,' croaks Jordan as he winces in pain.

All over, his peeling skin is now shades of green, grey, plus a reddish, thicker layer of fatal sun burn.

Clambering along a brick wall, Jordan's forced to limp, and stalk my carefully forged path, treading a thin line to avoid the raging fires, which have spread from the shop, then endorsed by the dying sun from up above. I try to keep one eye on him, but if I don't keep scaling this narrow line, we're both done for.

'I think it's radiation. I don't know what to say,' I inform him, spiritless. No energy left to afford the luxury of forming sentences hinged on positivity.

Still, I have to try, as it's really the least I can do. 'But trust, you will see them. You got this, brother.'

I then point us forward to Jade's Mum's house, miraculously still standing amidst the tall fires, blowing us backwards. I guess these lot get what they pay for. 'We've made it, J. Just a few steps.'

Our task is surprisingly easy, for when we hobble along this once seemingly perfect road, things actually run smoothly. A nice breather, for once.

We're used to it now, as this backdrop of devastation seems to feel like home. I ignore every other thought and attempt to squint so hard that the long driveway forming the entrance once again appears as pristine. Perhaps the slick, matte-grey Range Rover blocking our path helps to support that hypothesis. Jordan takes my hand, and I pull him through the narrow gap between the ash-burned hedges. He's almost blown away by the sporadic gusts of wind, striking us down, time and time again.

'We'll get you inside, and who knows, they might even have a hot roast ready for our arrival,' says my hunger, for me.

Jordan reacts with a rare grin, which means more than anything, especially regarding the context.

All feels restored, momentarily, when Jordan hits back with an even better line. 'I'm good, my bro, I'll starve. I know they won't be washing that chicken.'

His laugh is contagious, as it always is, and I'm only forced to stop when it worryingly morphs into a long, wheezing cough. He chokes up, his stomach clenched. I did warn him about laughing way more at his own jokes, over others. Bad karma, and all.

We reach the door, still in one piece, debatably. Whatever level of radiation we're at, it feels severe. Each invisible ray picking at Jordan's life source every second we're stood here, and I try to suspend my panic for when we make it inside. I knock, then bang on the front door, and repeat the process.

No answer. I'm unable to peek inside the blackout blinds of the front window and soon begin to worry. What if someone already came to their aid? It's surely a good thing, but also means they would have come and gone and there's no one left to find us.

'Grab my phone, call her. They have to be in here,' I tell Jordan. He's nodding off, unable to digest any information to preserve the minimal energy he has left. I echo my command, 'the phone, Jordan?'

Eventually, Jordan musters the will to deliver the news. 'It's broken. Cracked in my hand at the shop. I didn't even get to talk to her.'

He showcases the evidence, a painful long slash, cut through his palm, leaking with blood. I'm filled with a terrible wave of guilt when I study the wound, knowing that if my phone shattered before he could speak with Jade, then he's yet to find out.

'Before we get in, I think I need to say something, bro.' My voice, broken as it clashes against the wind.

Jordan scowls, sensing my confessional tone. When I do muster the courage, I'm beaten to it.

'WAH.' That monotonous cry can only originate from one known source. They're in the basement.

Urgency kicks in and directs us down to the basement door, beneath a steep flight of stairs. But first, we are forced to navigate our way past the four by four parked out front. Jordan rushes ahead of me.

That's when time reverts to slow motion.

Helpless, I watch the event unfold. It begins with Jordan squeezing by the car, just before he trips up.

Then triggers a moment of disaster. I'm slow to react but I know what's coming as soon as I watch the scene play out. My words, also delayed, are too slow to warn him.

'Jordan!'

They're unspeakable, the thoughts rushing through my head as Jordan swivels round, and we're face to face. An everlasting stare which coincides with the fatal blast.

The car explodes, and takes us with it.

I only narrowly escape the fallout, but this ferocious, inescapable fire latches onto my surroundings. With my ears ringing, and my vision masked by smoke, I fight my way through to feel Jordan's hand on mine. He's spread along on the floor, piled under a destructive heap of luxury car parts. Half of his face, it has visibly been blown off. But he's alive.

Emotions are forced to make way for practicality, I do my best to drag Jordan out of the wreckage, but am late to spot the worst of it, lodged inside of him.

Jordan falls in and out of consciousness, as I carry him backwards and down the stairs to the basement. The cries of the baby inside provide us a faint yet promising sign of the circle of life, which I shake off.

I place him down. 'JADE. Open up, Jordan's hurt!'

The sun sits closer to the earth than a low flying plane, its fire catching up to us, ignited by burning bushes and skeleton-trees that once looked so beautiful. A lot can change in twenty-four hours. All of it, in fact. Jordan slumps by the floor at the basement doorstep, leaving just myself to wedge it open. There's something firmly blocking our entry from the other side. Above all of today's events, now we need a miracle. My tears flow, as I pull the door.

With slow but determined strides, Jordan stands up and tracks back for a run up. Not that he's left with much space, stood mere inches away from the fires. I'm left without the ability to speak as he dashes forward, his broad shoulders spread wide as if squaring up against a bear, to run rapidly and collide with the door, and make it to the other side.

Jade's Mum greets us at the door, but not in the way I had pictured it. Her burnt, lifeless corpse forms an apocalyptic welcome mat, which frightens the life out of me as soon as I enter this corridor inside. I'm then forced to step around her, to scoop Jordan up from the floor and spur us onwards. The odour emitting from the body is one I'll never forget. Jade's Mum, she surely died protecting her daughter from whatever threat threatened them from the outside. Her front door is barricaded with all the chest and drawers a Dulwich house can fit, but the sheer power of today deems any type of metal or wood defenceless. I just wish I was there to help.

My thoughts are getting the better of me, as I've now completely miss Jordan's efforts to block the wind. With his back turned, I view Jordan's radiation-worn skin through the many holes in his shirt. That horror engulfs my expression now he turns to view me, his other front-facing half melting away, similar to the state of the flaming man, whose earlier demise led to Daniella's eventual death.

For whatever unjust, devilish reason, I just know it, I'll be the last one standing at this rate. This reckoning, it has Kyle written all over it. Less so the fires, and more so the wind, is the imminent threat knocking the both of us backwards. Amongst all the junk Jade's Mum used to guard her door with, is an industrial power hose. I rush to unravel it.

Jordan struggles to hold the door but still pushes on, despite himself, now knee-deep amidst the fires, with the basement doorway slowly giving in on him. This is not the time to freeze up. I rush over to assist him, as he has done so for me throughout today, and begin my battle with the wind, using the all-mighty power hose. We're not thinking straight, even though our survival demands it. This box of a basement will not hold its weight any longer, and I sense Jordan, thinking the same. I stand behind him, he shrugs me off then turns to grip both of my cheeks. When I look deep into his eyes, I feel the radiation seeping into my own veins. His face is now a paler shade than ever, even more so than a ghost.

Jordan snatches the hose from me.

I try to snatch it back. I won't let him leave me, but I also know, he won't let that stop him.

'You have to make it, for us!' Jordan's voice is subdued by the chaotic uproar of wind and fire.

Still, I refuse to let our saga reach its end, but Jordan shakes me off, and looks me dead in the eye.

'Jordan and Kyle, 'til the end. Love you, bro. Always.'

The apocalyptic sun meets its match. I watch Jordan courageously step past the line that splits the rest of humanity from the endless oblivion that has decided to descend upon us, clutching onto the power hose.

Our last shared action is a significant one, for when he blasts the water against the colossal gust of fire-powered wind back out to the world, steps outside to face it, and slams the main door behind him, I'm forced to open and close the one defending Jade's apartment, and gateway to the earth. The ultimate battle of the elements signifies the sad, melancholic path our reality has taken.

We part ways forever. That's when I reach my limit, and final destination.

Breakdowns are a word used to describe the many truly devastating, but arguably temporary, situations life can simply dump on us whenever we least expect it. I broke down when Vanessa left, when my cat died, or whenever boss man's out of white Kinder Bueno's.

But this moment, exactly what I feel right now, sits a tier above all. In the grand scheme of things, this is a grand scheme breakdown, from which there is no return.

No more Jordan and Kyle toasting a glass to their twenty-fifth birthdays, together. No more Jordan and Kyle doing up best man duties, marrying beautiful wives, then raising even more beautiful children, together.

No more Jordan and Kyle, period.

A consequence I thought I'd never have to face.

We went through it all today, but naturally, that last moment will leave an eternal stain on my memory. It's also one that amazingly resembles the first. Year seven, day six, almost the seventh, ironically the day our divine creator rested while his least remarkable creation was subjected to his biggest test. I faced the long B-Block hallway just after chemistry class, to face a horde of pocket-jingling Year Tens. Jordan then stepped in and crushed that storm, all because I just seriously smoked our teacher for mocking his limited knowledge of exothermic chemical reactions. Perhaps the most ironic fact today is, science is now the enemy, clashing Jordan and myself, an alliance formed by the strongest exothermic reaction known to man. The Year Ten's signified our shared demons.

I attempt to shake myself off from the tiring stream of consciousness triggered by losing him, and revert to the critical matters at hand, but struggle to do so. I sit there, eyes peeled to the hot floor, wailing away. A cry so awfully loud, caused by the ultimate loss of my closest friend, that it may only be matched by a feeling of equal weight. Which just so happens to be the case. A noise emits from the far corner, which permits me to think the unthinkable.

I have lost my best friend, but what if I have just gained another?

'WAH.' The cry rises in volume, from the baby.

One swift, upward glance brings me back into the room, to be faced with Jade's fierce gaze, dead-on. My eyes track downwards to see the kid in her arms.

Before I can even deep the significance of that cry, the dread kicks in. An emotion caused by my own choices and actions a long time ago, yet still too recent for me to have truthfully addressed it. The sun has beaten me down and tested me to the max, but fails to compare with my biggest fear, and rival. Myself.

'Where is he, Kyle?' Jade's first words to me are the hardest to hear. My blank expression says it all. 'Where is he? Where is Jordan!'

I rush over to her. Jade sinks her head into my chest. Her cry is silent, for there is no audible need to express her pain to the world. Not that planet Earth deserves it, having just taken Jordan away from us, plus the rest of our species.

Consoling Jade, my eyes scan this small living room, thinking to myself, this is it then, the end of the line. I do wonder, for whatever interplanetary historian does choose to visit us in the coming millennia, what might fascinate them more? A 4K flat screen mounted to the wall, or the tangible leftovers that remain of our lives and memories? I look to a basket full to the brim with baby formula and all of the other useful, or completely useless gifts from loved ones, including my own: a neat box of baby-sized Jordan 1's. An all too obvious joke.

My gaze lands on a photo of Jordan, hugging one of his many golden boot trophies, followed by Jade's Mum, one of the more selfless heroes of our times. Jill, her years spent in and out of social care homes, dedicating her life to those who needed it most.

Last, but certainly not least, I look back to the baby. Everything else seems to fade into the background. The sun and the outside apocalypse, the black hole in my heart vacuuming me into the darkest of voids, and the constant questioning of why this reckoning has gifted us more minutes that Mr. Old Man could ever have dreamt of. None of that seems to matter now that I am blessed with this sight, of new life. As the baby and I lock eyes, I allow it to creep in, my smile. The first, for a long time.

I feel Jade's lips on mine to bring me back to present and I wish, for the life of me, it was a surprise, alike Daniella's. Jade's touch is like no other, and I give in. Even the way my lips moulds around hers feels like home, back to a feeling all too familiar, yet all too regretful. My darkest secret, it resurfaces and consumes me now that there are no others, absolutely no one, not a soul, to hide it from.

In this moment, our gentle kiss carries with it all the complex and contradictory forms of human emotion that has marked the ridiculously special existence of our kind, right from the beginning. I'm not even sure the most controversial pop culture kisses, the likes of Luke Skywalker and his own sister, Princess Leia, can even come close to this.

I'm then reminded of how this secret uplifted me when Vanessa broke my heart by cheating on me, but completely plagued my mind for an entirety of the past nine months. Knowing I'm no better, for committing the exact same sin. Me, the guilt ridden perpetrator of the ultimate crime. But sleeping with Jordan's girl, Jade, arguably my worst lifelong choice, I'm somehow convinced, was also my best. That's what's so messed up.

'What do you want to name him, Kyle?' asks Jade.

I look to Jade, stunned, also filled with clarity. 'Jordan.'

Jade hands over Jordan, our new baby boy. Of course, it weighs on me with every second his heart beats, the dark nature of this deep and twisted reality. Yet at the same time, I've never felt so elated.

It was never supposed to be this way. Me, Kyle, alive, without any of them left. Without Jordan, Daniella, everyone at the bar, all dead, gone, and perished. Perhaps this reckoning was meant for me, I'm only still left here to pay the price. Not for just sleeping with my best friend's girl to get over a breakup, but then falling for her, hard. For going back time and time again in secret, when every inch of my body told me to stop, to confess, to make things right and tell Jordan that I am the one who gave his girl, the only one he could actually fall for, a baby. I didn't just stab him in the back with a knife, I stuck the samurai sword deep into his heart from the rear, twisted, and let it turn for nine endless months, whilst him, face to face, every single day.

Every minute along the way, I acted as if I couldn't ever be prouder to be his chosen Godfather, when I, knowing full well that I must be the father. Perhaps one day we, far in the future, may have reconciled after I spent four decades begging for his forgiveness. But now Jordan's no more, that will never happen. And for that, for a fact, I shall pay.

Truthfully, I deserve for this day to loop and replay a thousand times over. I'm staring down at it, at him, my kid, my genes, my own flesh and blood, the living, breathing product of my biggest betrayal. The worst part of it is, he's just too beautiful.

'What're you thinking, K?'

Jade's question may take some years for me answer. Time I simply don't have to spare anymore.

I decide to pay Jade back with the only thing I have left. That is, 'love. I'm filled with it, I shouldn't be but deep down, Jade, I know I'd do it all again. To finally see him, in my arms.' I confess.

Jade smiles wide, I'm smiling too. The pair of us beaming down at baby Jordan and his twinkling set of eyes. In this brief, yet everlasting moment in space and time, the three of us are, undoubtedly, the happiest family on earth. We even erupt to laughter, though we really shouldn't, when Jade realises that I've got my ugly, sun-burned, and radiation-ridden hand wrapped around our baby's finger.

To think I used to fear children. Whether a relative's birthday, wedding, funeral, or any other messy party hosted under the guise of a child's celebration, and I would be in and out, quick time. Trust me, I could avoid anything. If a niece sprints over to braid my hair, or a cheeky nephew kicks a ball to me, bet I'd run a mile from it. But I see it now.

I truly see myself in him. I also know that he could amount to so much more. A double edged sword, knowing he'll never get that chance.

With my gaze fixated on the slightest of movements from my baby, the spine shivers caused by the slowly creeping sensation of the cold, difficult truth, creeps in. It spikes as I spot the eclipse over his shiny, reflective brown eyes, being gradually overshadowed by red. The bold shadow of the low-hanging sun engulfs the room, cast directly through the window.

'I still just wish Jordan could have met him, you know,' states Jade. Incredibly unfazed by this whispering call to an apocalyptic death, she remains strong, for us.

So, I choose to remain strong for her, and say it, 'I could have told him the truth. I was too scared.'

Following my remark, Jade shifts away from the baby, to place a comforting hand on my left cheek. 'He knew. Jordan knew, K. I had to tell him, on the phone today, scared I'd never get the chance.'

Almost solely through the sure powers of her psychic touch, Jade gauges my reaction to the truth. I know she can feel it in my wavering wrinkle creases, that I'm instantaneously left speechless, surprised, shocked and above all, content. Jordan did know. He knew what I did, he truly knew me, Kyle, through to the core. But still, he sacrificed everything and risked it all, despite having every reason to do the opposite, and end me on the spot. Jordan made sure we fought until the end, together.

'So, the phone wasn't broken?' I ask, still stunned.

Jade avoids my stare, her stream of tears forming. 'He told me he loves me, and will always love you, even if you cat his style, and fell in love with his girl. Classic Kyle, typical, he said. You know how he is. Always joking, right up until the last minute.'

Just that makes me increasingly aware of two things. First. the impending sun, and the odd minute we have left. Second, are Jordan's last words, which mightily overpowers the first. Jade's upbeat tone reflects the infectious power that my best friend always had on others. Even after he's gone. Now we both cry, flooding tears of joy. Just how it should be.

Nothing, but simultaneously everything, are the few words I'll choose to describe our mood now that we are ready to approach this final chapter.

We both stand firm in a silent but mutual agreement that this end, it is ours. As Jade, our baby Jordan and I approach our shared conclusion, I believe it, that this is what makes all the difference.

Before today, I would have congratulated myself for being here to simply witness it. The end of the world, such a big, historic moment. Now that I'm actually faced with it, my overwhelming sense of satisfaction is purely in retrospect. I had a good ride.

Despite our reality, feeling helpless is far from it. A newfound energy fills me from head to toe, shielding Jade and our baby from the spellbinding red light outside. The sunlight invades the room at all angles, through the window, then the four walls, crashing down upon us. Clutching onto them both, I still cannot refrain from one last sneaky glance upwards, to watch the sun initiate its final phase and with it, comes the end of the line. The last act to the wonderful stage play that is humanity, and planet earth, as we know it. I'm engrossed by the blood-red sun, now just mere metres away from us. It's beyond any magnitude I'll ever truly grasp, a warmth like no other, its power so intense, it simply cannot be put into words. Not that I have any left.

I take my final breathe, one that's oddly filled with panic and peace alike, and take one last look at my new-born son, Jordan, before we join the sun on one last, momentous journey, and fade away along with it, to join it in the dark but ever so bright, twisted end that is so well known to us all, as death.

EDEN'S SONG

The decision to dress in exclusive all-black attire for this occasion has already achieved the opposite outcome to what was originally intended. To stand out, as a result of my intention to stand in, has well and truly sealed my fate way before my arrival. Even now, as I stand here immersed into a sweaty, claustrophobic crowd of today's proudest and most notorious societal outcasts, I'm left out on the fringes. Unlike them, I know what I am, yet forever question where I belong. But tonight, I must believe it so, that I do belong here, seeking for answers, just like them.

In front of me are the Pinks, behind stands the Blues. What would normally reflect the fixed, complicated lines between each of our beliefs, now stands for something else. Something special, like never before. We are united within our single purpose, queuing in anticipation, eager to see her for the first time. Still, that doesn't stop the peering eyes, all landing upon me. I make a decision to politely approach the Pinks.

Pinks are the punk-rockers of my age. Convincing, but detachable Mohawks, and leather-look jackets. Through their pink eye contacts, this trio stares me down. One laughs at my lack of anything, the other gifts me a loud pink cap.

'So, black's the new vanilla,' spits a bitter Pink.

I laugh, fitting the cap. 'Can you believe she's here?'

That line, a desperate plea for their brief acceptance, works. Three becomes four and although I'm aware, they've only acknowledged me to distance further from the Blues, my body a firm wall to their nemesis, I blend right in. Clueless but ruthless, it's all part of the act.

'You're right. MIA for so long. Had me worried we'd never get the chance,' says a perkier Pink, tiptoeing to assess the long line.

At the front of this dark, narrow tunnel stands a pair of bouncers, their arms crossed, wielding guns.

'What do youse think, then? You know, about the truth.' They eye me sceptically after that, my audacity to even question her power working to single me out again. I adjust, quickly, 'I believe it, but you know.'

The third Pink, initially the quietest, looks livid. 'And what would you know about a truth you're yet to experience?'

Unsure where to look after that, I stare beyond her. The kindest Pink of them all slaps me hard on the back and follows it with a smile. 'Same boat, love. It's why we're all here, right?'

I'm late to realise the gap left in his words, surely expecting me to fill it with my name. 'Right, Mara.'

A vibration rings from deep inside my ear, rising in volume the more I ignore it, to dampen my hearing. The bass rumbling the stone walls of the archway falls flat. Before I know it, I've missed something.

The brigade of Yellows has started on the Blues. A tense standoff until a tall bouncer arrives. 'Tickets?'

That fixes things. We all stand firm, an unflinching line of misfits unwilling to ruin our chance of entry. This is no normal event, in fact, it's a once in a life time thing, should the rumours hold any weight. The news would have you think the opposite, quite literally, but this show has been the talk of the town for months. Eden, known as the last living musician, hinges on the fact of urban myth.

I'm still doubtful it will go ahead, and I'm not the only one. The archway echoes with gossip-filled chatter, debating the theories over how we all may leave this tunnel, tucked far beneath the grounds of society, completely changed, except in all our own different ways.

Some are here for her, others are here to soul search, the common denominator is that we're here for the truth. That's all there is to know about her performances, they're said to be the key to unlocking it all. I'm here to find that out.

Once I watch that same bouncer finish his rounds and circle backwards to reach the front, his partner nods then reaches for a switch. As soon as he flicks it, the tunnel goes completely dark. Seconds later, a multicoloured glow sweeps throughout the floor beneath us. A sharp, rapid, twitching, neon rainbow.

Just like that, the doors at the head of this long line burst wide open.

'Single file! You will be asked to leave any photo or communications devices at the door upon arrival!' Both bouncers repeat the command as we swarm in. 'Welcome to the Down Under!'

I ride the wave inside.

When the archway flows inside and widens into the vast stretches of an enormous entrance, I stop against the tide of the stampede, to take in the sight of this warehouse ahead of us. The tirade of Pinks, Yellows, Blues, and every other group under the sun, all congregate around the different bars.

Gig-goers disperse into many, all shuffling forwards to receive the pints poured into jugs at the front. It's the first time I've seen human hands work that hard, but equally efficient, for a long while. Work they want to be doing makes all the difference. Beer jugs spill into overflowing cups when clinked between comrades of all colours. I rub my eyes in disbelief.

Within the centre of this huge hall, tables and stools make way for a dance floor which shakes due to the booming sound systems placed in each corner. It's all very old school, but surely not a replica and the more I notice each fine detail, the venue itself appears as if a dated relic, from a past long forgotten. Dating back to a time I should remember, but don't. Whether that be from all the late nights, after-parties, the foggy haze of my past, or maybe, it was *Them*.

Now, I'm cramped up against a stone wall, queuing for a pint to calm the anticipation and follow the status-quo. My eyes lock onto the faded words etched into the wall adjacent to me. Tracing my fingers along, when I touch it, I feel it.

'Inside yet?' screeches a voice from inside my own ears. The longer I leave it, the more danger I'll be in.

So, I get myself moving.

When steel, gunmetal cubicles swing open and close, the added stench of everything you would expect in here converges into one. I hold my breath as I wait for an opening. The dance has already erupted inside, and heads collide to cause a reaction of intense excitement, which bounces from wall to wall. I decide to butt in, an agenda to advance myself to the front as I jump on the spot to display a greater urge to piss compared to the others, also queuing up.

'Go on, let her through,' says the sympathetic Yellow in front of me. Normally, I'd decline anything that points to preferential treatment. But today, I need to play my cards right.

My plan is immediately effective, and I overhear the grunts from behind, which distracts me from the cubicle door in front. When it swings open, it almost slams me in the face. I watch a man drowsily exit, slim and unmistakably lanky with a fresh red buzzcut.

He catches the steel door then perks up to see me, and with that same wet hand, slaps me on the shoulder. 'Long time, eh!'

Foot in the door, I take a moment to ponder who the hell a Red may mistake me for, considering my plain black outfit and stupidly pink cap, before I enter the small the cubicle.

'Talk to me, Mara. I'm still waiting.' That voice from the inside, forcefully guiding me.

Reluctant, but also afraid of stalling any further, I choose to respond. 'She's here.'

What followed was a tremendous hour, one that felt prolonged in the best way possible. I got a lot done. Drinking competitions with the Pinks, set on the task of humiliating the Blues, only to begin dancing with them to bassline anthems. Genres I've only ever heard of before as whispered rumours were somehow being spun by those I never even knew existed. The Purples, also known as the Untouchables, and as I watch them up on that stage, spinning the rarest rounds of vinyl's that if sold would be an instant, but criminal gold-rush, I wondered if we ever crossed paths prior to this. Of course, in the grand, dead beaten upstairs of our dull society, that would be impossible to have known.

For some years, some more than I can remember or trace back to the initial point of which, it has been criminalised, corrupted, banned, and now, illegal. Those labels, one by one, stopped everyone fighting, with their families, friends, and in my case, careers, on the line. That being culture, in all its different forms. The one, essential thing that defined us now ceases to exist, because it would now cost each individual far too much to risk it all.

Except for here. Except for this movement that Eden has introduced to the world that, now, as it stands, it is stronger than ever. The colours are back out again. Perhaps not forever, and perhaps just below inside this warehouse of old-timer mosh pits, alcohol, and the mind blowing array of national foods we can only pray is etched into our memories. One night Down Under is, perhaps, just enough to give these people hope.

However, the ultimate fear, one that sweeps through the unsaid cracks of this well-hidden secret venue, is not the fear of being caught, nor the fear of in-fights. This fear, shared by all that I lay my eyes upon right now, as I explore what they call roti and bhaji stalls, feasting as if for the first time, is that all it takes is one brief moment for us forget. To forget any of this ever happened and then be dragged upstairs to our homes, unchanged, as if all of this never was.

This is known as a News-Flash, an old term for a dangerous new method. One that instantaneously wipes the five senses, plus any thoughts or feelings discovered in any chosen amount of time, forever. The by-product of which, is that a News-Flash makes its subject solely believe whatever memory is used to displace it. Although it first begun within the national news, making their political agendas all too easy to force down our throats as we watch their screens, it is now in the hands of the powers that be. The issue is, due to the excessive use of News-Flashes all round, no one knows who those powers may even be. Yet, they killed all our cultures.

Even more problematic, for selfish reasons, is my issue. The fact of my own personal life, erased, upended, then exploited for a new, unwanted, and certainly unspeakable career path. The worst part is, and I can't be sure, although I feel certain of it in this moment, before I am again forced to forget, is that I now work for them. *Them.* Still, my theory is a wild shot in the dark, especially when the last few years of my life has mostly been one big News-Flash.

Yet, right now, as I walk with a belly full of curry and a whiskey-filled cup of homemade ginger beer, I feel closer to my own forgotten long-lost passion. An odd but familiar sensation, and I'm sure of it. I may not remember the details of my past, but right now, even a News-Flash can't stop me. Similar smiles paint the faces of each gig-goer I pass whilst topping up my drink with no-label whiskey and, in a good way, I feel invisible, like I'm home. Liberated, even elated. That is, until I hear it again.

'What on earth are you doing?' This voice, which almost drove me to insanity until I learned to co-exist with it. 'You're here for one reason, get it done.'

I shake it off, ignore it and keep moving on in my bliss, but they won't let me. A sharp pain, stemming from my torso upwards, shoots up and stings me, badly.

A slap on the back of my head snaps me out of it. 'Been looking all over, ever since our slash.'

That buzzcut Red I encountered in the toilets. He's studying me, whilst twitching on the spot.

'Think you've mistaken me for someone else,' I say, focused on the sharp pain as I step away.

But he follows me. Even steals a sip of my drink, before slapping my back again which, oddly enough, dulls my brutal inner pain. He halts my steps to whisper, 'come, she's waiting.'

Conflicted, I stay put and watch him walk away. An internal pain pushes me forward, 'go!'

'We want truth! We want truth!' The chants of the crowd at the end of the warehouse tunnel, away from all the beverage stalls, edges closer and closer. The Red takes my hand, grips it tight, and slithers his way through the massive venue, passing by each group in the crowd, one by one, plus the huge stage towering from above.

We shoot into a backdoor, which leads to a small tunnel, and pass by many discreet groups, as well as a large crew of even larger bouncers.

The Red nods to them all and with a quick swivel backwards, he grabs me by my cheeks and pulls me in, almost kissing me, then eyes me.

He consoles me, 'it's all good. You're good, safe, you don't need to worry here.'

'Nice,' spurts my inner voice, always there, judging me. I wince at the thought, of following the Red inside, which also means to take it in with me.

After a cheeky wink from the Red, he turns back around, to face a black door in front of us.

He creaks it open and reverts to his hushed tone to announce, 'I got you a visitor, Eden...'

Speechless is the only way to describe the first moment I lay my eyes upon Eden. Fixing her transparent veil whilst clutching a black bottle of rosé, before she turns around. She's angelic, but in her demeanour, all too real. Both at the same time. An assistant stands close by, attending to Eden's every need as she elegantly sips from her bottle. When the assistant finally works the veil to perfection, I catch a glimpse of Eden's smooth buzzcut. A shimmery, metallic, rose gold.

When Eden finally acknowledges my presence, she waves off her assistant and sits propped up on the dressing room table, then drinks some more. I even shy away from her glare. Not one of us say a thing, not even a word.

Until the Red breaks the ice. 'Getting wild out there. Ready?'

Eden's gaze lands on Red and breaks into a light smile, accompanied by an assured laugh.

'Want some?' asks Eden as she extends her bottle.

Red reaches out for the black bottle and I'm left watching them like television, my thoughts fighting away the guilt knowing that they are watching, too.

'Her, not you. You want some drink?' Eden asks as she drifts over to my side of the room.

I fail to process what's happening, but soon snap out of it when Eden clicks her fingers at me. I'm losing control. I can tell when the drowsiness kicks in and leaves me late to my reactions. This peculiar sensation, it's the same as when I suddenly awoke in a queue behind the Pinks, earlier on tonight.

'Right. Thanks.' My words fail to match my actions and instead of reaching for the bottle, I stand, frozen.

Eden looks into my eyes, but somehow past them, and deep into my soul, whilst prodding the bottle into me. 'Trust me, it'll help.'

As I take a sip, and then another, I feel it leaving my body, the drowsiness. I look to her, surprised, as she smirks back.

'Where'd you find her, Red?' asks Eden, interrogative but playful in her tone.

Red stops stuffing his mouth with cashews. 'Feasting, right by the cuisines.'

I laugh down to my stomach at Red's remark. It's strange but for a few seconds, that sense of home, which has flirted with me all night, cements itself. When looking to them both, Eden, plus Red, a soft and slushy sensation seeps into my mind, and it's a relief. Reminding me of a time when I used to laugh. I just knew Red would act a fool and when Eden shuts him down, I also knew that one was coming.

After another swig, I assess the bottle. 'Strong shit.'

That clarity only lasts momentarily. They always manage to find a way, and I feel myself slipping. Increasingly dazed as the seconds pass, I feel numb. My sense of self, now evaporating. I'm forced to take a backseat, and in the spur of the moment, I grab Eden with force, catching her off guard, and I collapse. Eden swoops down to hold me before I can hit the hard floor of the warehouse room, she lifts me up, gently caressing the back of my head.

'I got you. Not long now, for your truth.' Eden's soft whisper soothes my peripheral, as I leave this realm.

The rest of this memory, meeting the one and only symbol of colour, of hope, is left blank.

All black, like most of my memories.

Just like my clothes.

When my eyes flicker open, I'm afforded no time to adjust to the change in my surroundings. The same room, the same company, but completely different. Red towers above my body, his left arm strapped across my chest to pin me down, whilst choking me out with his right.

'You can stop now,' hisses Eden, 'Red!'

Still panting, Red removes his arm, staring me down like the enemy, and perhaps that's what I am.

Wheezing, I gather my things, spread out along the cold floor. My wallet, a camera I sneaked inside, my keys and, well, something I didn't know was there.

I panic, trying to find the words. 'I swear I didn't. I, that, it wasn't me. I can explain.'

My hand lingers over it, Red picks it up. The gun.

'You didn't hurt us.' Eden's words are calm, and she looks generally unfazed by whatever occurred in the window of time I blacked out, but her tone has shifted. Fierce, almost disappointed as she turns away to apply the final touches to her outfit, occasionally watching me through the slither in her reflection. 'Showtime, Red. you know what to do. I can't leave them waiting forever. That isn't fair.'

Red pockets the weapon. I watch on, dazed, and confused when he conceals his jacket as he does so.

Eden eyes me again through the mirror. 'Keep an eye on her, Red. The show must go on.'

Red picks me up, pushes me to the door. I shove him off but join him to exit. 'What happened in there?' My voice is shaky guilty, despite knowing it wasn't my fault.

'Like she said, don't worry. Forget about it,' says Red, walking on. But I stop walking.

Red turns back around, irritated. 'You tried to kill her. I stopped it. Happy now?'

The long corridor leads us back towards the stage and the crowd, and weighs heavy with tension between myself and Red. He despises me now, and I don't blame him. But I can also tell that he's the type to stick to Eden's orders, no matter what. I admire that.

So, I'm safe. For now.

'Eden! Eden!'

Simultaneous cries rumble the venue as we slip far into the crowd. Back row seats. When I scan around to assess it, I come to notice, this crowd is on a literal high. That's when Red shoves me again, extending that same bottle I spot being passed back and forth by Greens, Pinks, and Blues, alike.

'Before you lash out again. Drink up.' His words are more of an instruction, than a friendly gesture.

Minutes later, I'm still sipping and soon I notice, the voices are gone, which gets me thinking. Am I really the doomed, enslaved secret spy I think I am, or is that the result of manic withdrawals, or perhaps loneliness? The more time I spend within this crowd, my vision spinning out while the other senses awaken and this euphoric high overcomes me, I feel like I do belong. The chants rise and finally, I join in, now that Eden touches the stage...

She's completely different in her aura to the Eden I had just met. I look to my right, a lightheaded swivel delayed by each delectable sip, to laugh with Red. But he's no longer there. Numb, high, and uplifted by my fellow gig-goers left and right, I simply sway on my feet as if I'm stepping on clouds.

The scene is set and so, the show begins.

Firstly, the room goes silent, the lights dim, we could practically hear a pin drop. But, nothing.

Soon a spotlight shines and surprises us all. As the piercing light beam shoots down to reflect off of Eden's golden buzzcut and passes through her veil, I feel as if she's looking directly at me. A quick glance around says that we're all feeling the same.

Incomes a haze of smoke from the stage, a sweeping mist that fills it with vibrant colour. Red, blue, pink, purple, and soon all of them combined. That's when Eden grabs the microphone, a solid gold object that dangles low from the high ceiling on a transparent lead, to finally break the silence.

'We're two out of three. Keep fighting 'til we're free.'

Anticipation is certainly an understatement here. We're enthralled. Myself in particular, high to a new level. That's when I spot Red, up on stage, trailing along with a golden saxophone, to hand it to Eden.

This is no normal concert. Any of those black market files going round in the old days could never match the calibre of this, now that I'm witnessing it unfold live. Eden's presence is one of a kind, it forces a transcendent shift in consciousness, so they say. Let's just say, they were right.

When Eden plays the sax for a simple, tear-jerking symphony of soft but penetrative tones, the mist that clouds the stage fills with notes. Real, tangible notes. They're like images, abstract illusions that grow then roam above the crowd and fade, but never without leaving their mark. Different notes of various colours float above my head to travel and sit above different sections of the crowd. Each gig-goer they land upon is instantly transfixed, their expressions shifting.

Some notes clash, some merge, and as they collide, then join forces and bounce away to separate again, that's when the melodies are brought into the world. It's almost as if Eden's playing fifty songs, all at once.

I'm already wiping the tears from my face by regularly removing my arms, interlinked with the others that surround me. We join forces and when Eden blows faster to increase the momentum of her play, the tune rises to become one so much more complex and so much more breath-taking, that life itself ceases to exist. The crowd is lost in the song. As one.

That's when Eden's song begins. She grabs the microphone. Her low-pitched hums converge with the saxophone and its high-frequency vibrations, for powerful high-notes to blend with soulful moans. The overall product is nothing short of mesmerising.

Eden's singing erupts without words, but at the same time, she's saying it all. Her voice touches the golden microphone and soon disperses into the same type of vibrant illusions which coast by and follow on, into the crowd to join their predecessors. Raw melodies grow to rich harmonies before they develop, evolve, and add further layers to the musical eco-system being created inside this warehouse.

Each minute forces a surprise, one that flips the form. Eden switches between long high notes and shorter murmurs, emitting sounds no longer than a word or two, whilst playing the sax as she strolls, from left to right. No emotions are spared, nor are opportunities missed to constantly reinvent and simultaneously innovate, every time she delivers.

The result of which, is a deep trance. A certain type of synergy achieved that is usually unthinkable in today's time of divide and conquer. The tunes are still roaming through the growing, colour-filled mist, to explore every small corner and avenue of the crowd, allowing Eden to walk with the mic. She approaches the front row and thanks them, hands to her chest.

Eden focuses on a girl in the front row, in tears. Now she's asking the girl, 'your name is?'

It's a Green she's speaking with. Infatuated, her voice trembles when shouting upwards. 'Val!'

All of us silently observe Eden, now taking Val's hand, who's in awe. 'Let us find your truth, Val.'

Jazz-like hums are sent by Eden into the crowd, a slow note that splits into a deep green haze then coasts above Val and remains fixed. Raised voices are hushed as we see the abstract become concrete when tangible, lifelike images are formed. The first shows Val marching down a road, the second shows her up on a podium at a rally, speaking to countless likeminded protestors.

Then, before our own eyes, Val is awakened, holding up a green bandana and finally giving it meaning. A purpose revived, as we come to see it, the green showing more than just a colour. It is now a fighting spirit, and just as a third image crops up, it is revealed what for: the climate.

'They don't even want us to fight for our own planet, our home. That's what you did, Val, every single day before they wiped your slate clean, to have you work in some fucking factory, and help destroy it.'

Gasps turn to claps, but Eden silences the crowd, then roams to the opposite end, to address a Pink. Those same Pinks, from the one who grilled me to the one who gifted me my pink cap.

'I've been watching you guys. In fact, I know you, and you knew me. Until they broke you down.' Eden follows those words with a wonderful pink note, which fills the mist. A new round of images form, showing these Pinks in their past glory days. Together, they danced, sung, created.

After which, the Pinks break into a performance. One of them sings, and Eden matches their high-pitched tone, whilst the others dance, with great skill. Finally, they remember. No longer ignorant to the source of their own pride and joy. A lifestyle long forgotten, is now recovered.

'We've all been robbed. That's why you're all here! But make no mistake, I'm the same as you. I myself have been robbed, and what lies dearest to my heart was also stolen. But I didn't let them take me, what defines me, a gift I'm grateful to extend to us all, on our shared mission.'

Eden's speech radiates and resonates, she matches it with an intense speed of vocal ad-libs.

One by one, individuals in the crowd are spellbound by the images that pop up above them, through the mist, to unveil who they once were.

The more Eden continues this song, and her speech, reaching down to touch hands with these gig-goers, the entire warehouse scene becomes increasingly animated. Loud sections of the crowd break off and explode into their own parties. Various groups sing, dance, shout and shake hands to not only meet for the first time, but also re-introduce themselves to others they have known for a while but were forced to forget. Confidently exchanging their real names, passions, occupations and living for the moment, a hope inspired by Eden. This must be what it was like; our lives, before the News-Flash.

People, re-discovering their personal lives and truths. There I am, though basking in this concert in great disbelief, yet still, wondering if I'll ever find mine.

The momentum for each different song reaches an all-time high, spread along this monumental crowd, again taking us to new heights. The party kicks off. I begin to loosen up, still transfixed but outwardly showing emotion, as is everyone else. Some are engaged in dance-offs, most are simply fist pumping the air, eyes closed, spoiled for choice when it comes to beats or melodies. Some even kissing one another. Chaos has reached full pelt, and what a sight it is.

Now, closely guarded by Red, Eden embarks on a new journey, trailing down from the stage. Bouncers close in and surround her, but no one dares attempt to defy the rules and touch her or disturb the peace.

Naturally, my own path of exploration has taken me quite far in, to truly immerse within the crowd and involve myself within the many passionate activities. Yet, the more Eden and her entourage weave their way through this crowd, stopping every now and then to shake hands and join the countless circles in front of them to sing, dance, and celebrate, I come to notice something. My heart stops at the thought, and I slow myself down, realising that Eden's surely searching for something, for someone. I cannot shake the gut feeling inside, that it must be me.

That golden microphone is the real life of the party. As it sweeps and ventures along the crowd, dangling from the ceiling, pausing for others to sing into it or confess their truths, it stays on course with Eden. Making its way until it dangles a mere metre away from my position.

Following which, an entirely new development unfolds, and to the surprise of many, the music stops. Aware that Eden is already heading towards me, I stop dead in my tracks, then instinctively step towards the microphone, to await her arrival.

'Quite the time we are having tonight. The best yet.' Eden's words spring from the microphone into the room with limitless energy, transfixing us all. Now spellbound, the room falls silent, except for the shifty push and shoves of those trying to get a good view of us both. Eden's gaze is fixed on mine.

Eden's tone is assured. 'For the first time, I feel as if The Down Under is finally doing the good work that what was originally intended for it. That is, to emancipate our souls through heart and joy. I may be the one to trigger this effect but it's you, the people, who give it meaning.'

I gesture a silent clap, as do the others embracing this speech, despite my nerves rising by the second.

'But what I'm about to do next, for all of you to truly experience, is something that will shed light on the importance of our pursuit for true freedom. Another example of how much they, those harsh powers that be, have taken away from our memories, our culture, and how much work there is to still do.'

Eden stops, then takes a step further in, and finally, she addresses me. 'What's your name?'

My time has finally come, and I'm terrified. 'Mara.'

Eden laughs the second I say it. I didn't expect that. 'No. No it isn't.'

Completely drawn in, the crowd also laughs, as one. Except myself, left isolated in the middle.

'Mara, meaning death. That's the name they gave you. Mara tried to kill me earlier, just minutes before our show tonight. But please, don't blame her. I don't. That's the life they gave you, Mara, as their cold-blooded snitch, as an assassin of sorts. But you're not crazy, you never were- well, maybe a bit- but all you can remember is being used by *Them*. To spy, to observe, infiltrate and kill, all to use your past expertise of culture, against you. All for their benefit.'

With each word, it all comes flooding back. The countless days and nights I spent creeping through dark alleys, stalking people up and down the city to snitch, report and when it really got bad, murder them. All for nothing. Innocent people, and I ended so many of them.

Just when I thought it couldn't get any worse, I look up above, and begin to see it. A note sung by Eden, sharp, piercing, and awful in tone, within a deep black mist, hanging over me. Clear, vivid images on display, of my dark, murderous actions. My lost memories, for all to see.

The gasps that follow are almost theatrical. Even though I feel the weight of those times, every single day I wake up, I was made to forget they were all too real. I have already cried tonight, tears of joy. But now, my tears are cold, and filled with devastation.

'Long, sleepless nights. Countless days spent talking to nobody. Not a soul, except for the voices stuck inside in your own head. The voices, though you couldn't be sure of it, of *Them.*'

I knew it. Those moments before I step out of my door, only to be hit with a momentous News-Flash. Now gently taking my cheek, Eden draws me in.

'But you had a life before this, a life they took from you,' Eden looks deep into my eyes, my very own being. The same as before the show.

'And the worst part of your torment, the torture they put you through, is that you don't even know why. Do you? You thought, who would agree to this? And that's what really haunts you. The why.'

I feel the hatred building around me, and rightfully so. But Eden gently takes my hand, to ward off the hostility. 'You did it to protect those who you shared a life with, the ones you lived for. Robbed of your own life, your own purpose. That was the ultimate crime.'

While the rest of the crowd look up to the mist and watch it unfold, the film of the life I lived before today, where my crimes replay, I feel assured, I no longer need to suffer through it. My gaze is fixed on Eden, hers too, and soon my tears pass to make way for a new emotion. The intensity of which rises, almost unbearable, but certainly unbreakable, when she emits a softer, subtle note, one I've heard before. Except it is no note. In fact, it's a name. My name.

'Repeat it. Announce it. Tell me, tell us your name,' instructs Eden, prodding me, guiding me.

I take my time, then let it spill. 'Joy. My name is Joy?'

Eden, now tearful, nods as she squeezes my hand. 'Yes, Joy. The one they stole from me.'

I remember.

It's been pent up inside of me for years, however long it's been, an emotion fuelled by the one that kept me going. The desire for freedom, to go home.

Just as I lean in further, meeting Eden halfway for her to hug and embrace me, the crowd reacts to the gold mist forming above us, where all colours unite. A mist morphing into a collage of bright, spellbinding memories, to show the bond once formed between myself and Eden. From the day we met, to all the amazing times that followed, days and into the day we got married…

Astonishment meets clarity the more I remember. At last, I am reunited with my truth. My person. Eden, stood right in front of me all along. Our memories flood the vibrant mist. The good, the days of bliss, and the bad, when they banned our right to be together, but we fought for ourselves, regardless. Eventually, when the room processes the shock of this revelation, the crowd rejoices, as do I. Those around us chanting, celebrating this climatic event.

Until, unfortunately, as with all the good things in this era, my peace within is soon outlived. The dopamine hit of my true, long-lost inner peace, leaves for a numb, anxious, disorientation.

My internal paradise, triggered by finally being able to re-experience the wonders of my own life, before it was robbed and repurposed for the gain of others, battles with another internal force, of danger. It's all too familiar. I retreat inside myself once again and lose control, just when things got good. I thought they were gone, and I was cured, but this must have been their plan all along.

Eden spots it too, as I fail to fight it, taking centre stage to fulfil its agenda. She knows she's too late.

The powers that be, using me as their vessel, swiftly move my body to grab Red, who faces the crowd in front in celebration, and yank the gun I sneaked into this guarded venue, from his front jacket pocket. Red loses balance as a result and watches on, defenceless, as I point the gun at Eden.

The dramatic gasps from the crowd return, this time with a fearful shift in tone. The unit of bouncers close in on and draw their weapons, aiming down their sights. Until Red swoops in and stops them.

Overwhelmed by the pain shooting upwards and into each and every one of my limbs, this stinging sensation, their way of keeping control, shoots me back into the depths of my mind.

Eden stands static within the centre, clearly wondering how her gift so quickly ceased have an effect. All the while, as I fall prisoner to my darker side, I'm left asking myself the exact same question.

The stand-off commences, whilst the oppressive force within me takes the microphone. 'Party's over.'

Once again, Red extends his arms to signal for the bouncers, armed and closing in on us, to stay put.

'Party's just begun,' says Red, surprisingly relaxed. 'Well, what are you waiting for?'

This is it. The time for me to put my all in, for good. In reality, to the spectators, I am the real villain here. After all, it's my finger on the trigger aimed at Eden. But on the inside, the truth is that I am a helpless soldier, left with no choice but to trigger an internal war. Emotion is my real weapon, as I fight from within. My veins pop through my trembling fingers, gripping the gun. I'm wielding my all, everything I've got, every memory, every day and night spent working for an evil force to no end, every moment of peace ever stolen from me, to regain my control.

Still, it's an impossible task. It almost works, and in what would appear as a split second to the others in the room, was a perpetual struggle of mine, to force my all into this shared consciousness, and win. Only to then fail.

I watch my own finger wrap firmly around this gun and squeeze it tight. When I move to pull the trigger, to shoot Eden, I spot her expression, for the first time in my life, now showing fear. I'm about to shoot my own wife.

Yet, the gun doesn't shoot. Nothing leaves the barrel. No sound nor bullet comes out the other end. Paralysed, the crowd realise too. Red laughs, dropping the bullets stored in his hand. He wasn't bluffing.

The bouncers surround Eden and block her off from my view. I drop the gun to the floor. Soon all eyes turn towards the exits which, one by one, are kicked in by the boots of stealth troops.

Reinforcements. The ones I must have called in earlier tonight, against my own will, before the show. The guilt of it, knowing that they were waiting on the moment I stood with Eden. That itself is nothing but another lost moment of the past, added to the long, murky grave pile.

Although I'm still fighting against it, my efforts are strained. The more members of the crowd I observe being surrounded and restrained, pinned down for violent arrests, that fact becomes clear.

Their plan has worked, the original mission to close in on The Down Under once and for all, using my naivety and eagerness to change, as an insider, is unfolding before my own eyes.

But Red grabs the microphone, to address us all. 'We knew you lot would turn up uninvited.'

My eyes land upon him, and with another wide grin, Red says calmly, 'that's why we prepared.'

The spotlight cuts out and the venue is plunged into darkness. I spot the fast moving shadow of Red, wielding the microphone in his hand to then face me, and swiftly knock me over the head with it, to take me hostage to wield off the other troopers.

Guns point at us from all angles, from both sides.

'You're right. It is over. We'll take back what's ours,' Red croaks into the mic, whilst choking me out, forcing my split consciousness to weaken.

I just about hear Eden through my peripheral. 'Red, do it now!'

The last thing I spot is Red, stood above me as he opens his jacket to reveal a device. Makeshift wires stitched into a piece of kit like a custom car engine.

Red tightens his grip on my neck, and squeezes, then reaches into the back of my head to grab two things. The first, being another type of wire, one I never even knew existed, he quickly reels it out from inside my ear. The second, is a strange, miniature, revolving disc, right at the end of it.

My eyes roll to the back of my head when Red yanks the disc out and races to catch the wires, to then plug into his own device.

He removes his jacket to reveal it. The bomb.

Through the sleeves of Red's jumper lies a small trigger. He closes his fingers around it.

As my eyes drift to a close, the final act I am to witness before I pass out is Red, pressing the button.

Time hits a standstill, and the various groups of partygoers, soldiers, bouncers, and the colour-sporting, cultural warriors of our past society, all come to a sudden halt. They know what's coming.

The moment I give in is also the moment of detonation. Another blackout, this time a complete shutdown.

One that happens to be a system reboot, of myself.

The events that followed within that window of time, I am quick to learn as I come to and finally do wake up, will forever be the stuff of legend. History being written, as intended, inside the Down Under.

I jolt awake to see that I'm in Eden's arms, and she's in motion, as are the rest of the warehouse crowd. A glance around in my dizzy disorientation reveals the aftermath of events, following Red's bomb. Troopers line the floor, their prisoners breaking free. When I spot the eyes of the troops, my fellow, or now my former colleagues, rolling to the back of their heads, it becomes clear what has just unfolded.

Still, I have to ask. My eyes have deceived me before. 'What did he do?' My voice is faint, weak.

Eden looks down to me and slows her pace. 'He did it... We did it. We finally got them back.'

Soon enough, the crowd of gig-goers, turned rioters, and liberated persons who are each the beneficiaries of Eden's truth and Red's bomb, part to allow us through the doors of the warehouse. To exit in this fashion reminds me of tonight's journey, entering these very same doors as a silent nobody with a bleak agenda to end this movement, once and for all. Now, as we leave, and I'm the opposite.

Eden stops, and the others eavesdrop. 'One big News Flash. Wiping the slate clean, using their weapon against them.'

Eden lays me down to continue her speech. 'That's why you did it, you joined them, trusted them, so they trained you, and trusted you. But now, like you said, they'll have to start from scratch.'

The crowd around us hits an applause as if it was all part of the show, a dramatic payoff that wouldn't be complete without one thing. A final resolution, ending on a note of hope. When Eden kisses me, I remember it all. The plotting, the planning, the years of sacrifice that went into this day. The ultimate victory at the ultimate cost, but overall, I know one thing. That it was worth it.

Together, these liberated souls, societal outcasts who were once the pillars of past culture, watch mine and Eden's kiss form a note. The mist, a cloud of all colours, travels back inside.

Then, the doors of the Down Under burst open, hopefully for the last time, for we must hide no more. Outcome the troops, those who were also robbed of their own livelihoods. Like myself, all slaves to those ominous powers that be, no more. Now that they exit those doors to join us, I spot that look in their eyes. That feeling of freedom, of finally being able to go back home. Back to their families, friends, and ultimately, the lives they were made to forget on a daily basis. All from different walks of life which, now I remember, was the reason I built this place. The Down Under, it was my way of remembering. Way back, before I, myself, chose to go undercover.

'They can try to stop us, but we won't let them. Today is ours, no matter what.' My words sweep and morph into a wave of cheers from the crowd, and at last, it finally comes back to me.

My purpose, the same as my given name, of inspiring Joy. In the struggle and now, in the fight.

I look back towards the warehouse, thinking of Red, who sacrificed himself to carry the fatal implosion caused by the blast, a consequence of his ultimate task to reverse the News-Flash, and free us all.

I expend all of my strength to climb on top of our getaway van.

'To Red!' I bellow to the thousands in front, with my gaze now fixed on Eden, 'and to the revolution!'

We drive away, leaving The Down Under behind to fulfil our shared mission, and they follow.

COMMERCIAL ROAD

Back against the wall, slumps the long shadow of a man in a bomber jacket, busily vaping with baggy eyes. Locals sneak a peek at Mack as he bops his head to the tune of his own hums, with both of his eyes fixed on the entrance doors to this once-pristine local supermarket.

The tacky LED entrance flashes green. Mack spots his opportunity, in the form of a tiny old woman shuffling alongside her auto-trolley. Just a measly two-second gap is left by this woman, trailing off back to home, where the trolley will be awaiting her arrival.

That gap is beaten by zero point three seconds, futile against the speed of a man who knows the system all too well. The door closes in and Mack swoops in beneath it, as if to pay homage to one of his greats. Indiana Jones. Cue the smirk.

With a snap of his fingers, a flash of red illuminates the long aisle and Mack waits by a blind spot, just before he darts past an abundance of tech to finally find what he's looking for: a fresh, clearly discounted, classic pair of wired headphones. The product looks to be floating amidst its transparent packaging, and there's a flash of excitement in Mack's eyes as he studies each detail. He clearly wants it. Transfixed as if the product is speaking to him, and only him. That would be funny, until it isn't.

'Unfortunately, Mack, you cannot afford this product at this current time. Please check back again soon!' chimes the pair of headphones, just as he tries them on.

Mack's already off, cursing into the air as he boots over a wet floor sign, along his way through the supermarket. If only this place still employed workers to address this man and his kicks. That shit's a weekly affair. He surveys the shelves packed with plastic meats and expected overload of all things sustainable, yet all unattainable. Still, he's not one to give up that easily.

Sweeping through the shop in a far from casual stride, Mack's flow is soon interrupted by the upbeat sandwich clutched tight in his grasp. 'Are you sure about this purchase? Your credit count is extremely low.'

Mack nods, acknowledging the fair point, with his attention now afar, and fixed on an advert. Not for any kind of offer, but to squeeze in a free laugh, whilst squinting at the small print.

The advert shuffles away to captivate someone else who may be privier to its tag lines, as the algorithm morphs to suit their needs. He times the delay as the headphones morph into dumbbells, a definite dig he refuses to not take personally.

Mack continues on, reaching the tills to scan his lunch, only to be met with an intrusive flash of red.

'I'm sorry, we cannot allow you to make this payment. Please check back again soon!'

The odd, brown breaded, neon green-filled sandwich is left crushed and abandoned, spilling out onto the floor. Mack considers another defiant kick of the machine, though he's wary of the CCTV, haunting him from behind. He glimpses his stalker, matching his pace to finally catch up once he flashes that award-winning face, of resentment, straight down the lens. He's braced for it, the flash of red that signals another penalty, followed by a piercing siren. Mack squeezes his eyes shut, both fingers to his ears, but, nothing. The door flashes green.

At last, a lucky break. Now back outside at that familiar brick wall, Mack pats his pockets to fetch something inside of them. Wearing a smug expression, he dashes away an old, broken set of tangled earphones afar, and his smirk grows now that he's finally in with the new. Those new headphones. The ones he can't afford.

'Incompatible model. Please upgrade to pair!'

Mack reverts to his default setting, with an expression that blends emptiness with rage. Eyes to the sky to glimpse the only natural living thing left, also wondering when they will inevitably take that away from him, too. But, just like everyone else, he's got his ways of coping.

As Mack concentrates on a long breathe and slowly counts down from ten, it becomes clear. Meditation, perhaps the only thing saving that whole, entire supermarket from lighting up in flames. Slowly, Mack drags his feet away from the shop, to return back towards home.

Inside Mack's studio flat, there isn't much to see. Studio is rather a lavish term for this square box of a room, cornered off with a rusty old sink and toilet that connects to a basic excuse of a kitchen. Of course, he's enrolled on the bronze package, which covers the basic necessities. Mack's spread along his squeaky single bed that doubles as a makeshift sofa, beneath a wall religiously lined with 90's film and rap posters. His idols watching TV with him.

Projected through his mobile phone and onto the wall, old re-runs of *The Walking Dead* provide the necessary escape. He's reached the crux of a climatic face-off. The entire community is at stake, and only Rick Grimes stands against it. That's how Mack sees this world, as well as himself. He would argue, he's not the one out here crushing communities, those are the actions of one particular entity. He would also argue that he isn't any kind of hero.

These kinds of thoughts are the comfort Mack seeks when watching such re-runs. Though made to feel like a villain, or a thief, he knows deep down, he's neither one. He's just trying to exist, in a city where that is now, apparently, extinct. The city of London, where the gates eventually gave way to let in a horde of mental zombies.

As expected, a national news bulletin, from the ultimate authority that sits above all, soon invades every one of Mack's screens. What used to at least wait until evenings for families to congregate after work and school, is now a daily ritual.

It was much easier when 'they' were a type of nameless myth excused as a crazed conspiracy, but now Mack knows exactly where to aim his sights.

His fixation on the enemy equates to a daily test of sanity, and most of the time, it's not even worth the mental price. Time is no longer free, and today, nor is the enthusiastic headline.

'After much anticipation, we are thrilled to announce it's finally here! The U-Phone XXX, X. Proudly brought to you by Ad-National!'

That is then followed by a long list of false promises, most of which Mack fails to hear. Archival clips and city-size shop queues take the floor, creating a stimulating experience that even has Mack on the edge of his seat. His mouth agape in anticipation of this latest product packaged in a sleek box, which is slowly being unveiled. That part, the unravelling, is admittedly, Mack's weakness. Just as it arrives, another advertisement interrupts, appearing so prominently that it's hard to see anything else, except for the visuals of protein shakes. Just another reminder to upgrade his rent to silver, as if that were possible, in any shape or form.

Mack stops himself from the brink of frustration and launching his phone against the wall. Instead, he resigns to an empty, meditative stare at the ceiling, listening to the mash up of protein visuals and news bulletins that clash for his attention. His phone trembles when he's finally able to zone out, accompanied by a classic rap tune ringtone. He lets it play, bobbing his head and lip-syncing the uplifting

Ice Cube lyrics, only to be made to remember, someone's actually trying to reach him. That's a first.

'Good morning. Am I speaking with Mack?' asks a polite voice, with crystal clear clarity.

'Who's this?' Mack bluntly responds.

The voice doesn't miss a beat. 'Mack, this is Sam. Just checking your availability. A sudden opening in our schedule means we're able to bring your interview forward!'

Mack fixes his posture, processing those words.

'We'll front all travel expenses,' interjects Sam.

Mack circles his flat to ward off his rising heart rate, but there aren't enough corners to stall him any longer. 'Course. Where?'

Sam states, 'You'll find our UK offices within the Business District. Will twelve noon today work for you?'

Mack taps his feet anxiously, agrees to see Sam and thanks him for the opportunity, masking a smile.

Sam responds, 'Thank you, and you will not see me. This is an automated call.'

'Why Sam, then?' asks Mack, his eyebrows raised.

'Systematic Availability Maintenance,' states Sam, 'and Mack, punctuality forms the core of our company values here. Arrive even a minute past the agreed time slot, and we're left with no choice but to offer it to someone else. Understood?'

The call ends abruptly, leaving Mack confused about what just happened. Pondering each detail he forgot to enquire about. Definitely caught off guard.

Excitement follows and Mack rushes to get ready, strapping on a shirt and fixing his tie, before one last glance at his chaotic living space, which serves a strong dose of extra motivation.

As he slams the door and ascends off into the world, the mixed feelings begin to creep in already. This desolate, grey area of London is both home and a source of love and hate for him, but he's better than this, surely. That thought, guiding each step as he attempts to recall which of the several companies he reached out to within the Business District, that this may even be.

Still, the opportunity of an actual job interview is a dream come true for Mack, he's never had the chance. He ponders the odd occurrence of the invitation, but the task at hand is to venture into the Business District, a place he has never been able to afford, nor dared to ever visit. Nobody does, at least not from around here. Today is the day, and just like his permanent choice of ringtone serves to remind him, today could, in fact, also be a good day.

That optimism is fully embraced by Mack, glimpsing the sight of his neighbours, locked into their headsets, conversing with one another through their walls. He edges towards the end of his road to reach his prized possession and truly embark on this journey. A wide grin as the image forms in his mind of gliding into the city, and all the opportunities that may await him on the other side. But first things first, Mack retrieves his keys, and approaches the bike rack to unlock his fixed gear, the one thing he's proud to be able to call his own.

Of course, this time it's empty. The entire rack, dismantled, and Mack's bike, missing on today of all days. With livid rage, Mack kicks at the rack, but stubs his toe. He takes a small breath to let the anger subside but fails to keep it at bay. He's already started slow, and with a creased forehead and clenched knuckles, he searches for an alternative. Even the adjacent rentals have been raided.

Mack has no choice but to journey by foot, which is costly. He looks at his watch, not for the time but for a display of currency. Luckily, at that same time, Sam tops up his credits. Two credits become seventeen, with a wink-faced smile to accompany Sam's text message. Mack eyes it, half in disbelief.

The Nature District, it's the only option that lies ahead of him. Mack reluctantly passes the automatic toll, already deducted his initial two credits for even considering this route. An intercom startles him with a familiar voice to that of the supermarket, this time with added charisma.

'Welcome to the Nature District! We hope you enjoy your leisure time. Headsets are available upon request at a five credit hourly rate.'

Mid-jog, Mack takes a moment to soak up the free entertainment of the few civilians surrounding him. He observes a scene of war, commencing between two boys in camouflage tracksuits, engaged in their odd, bug-eyed, virtual reality lenses. They take cover as the first kid dodges a headshot, then continue to defend their cause. Reminded of his own childhood spent here, Mack smiles, thinking of the long summers spent chomping on of choc ices with whoever turned up to play out. Way back, when this was a real park, within a place called Peckham.

Next up, is the distracting sight of an elderly man, who runs at a snail's pace to intercept a ball that isn't there. He kicks at the ground, then celebrates, as if he's scored the last minute winner for a cup final at Wembley. Perhaps he just did since an applause hits from all over. The non-existent crowd are in uproar.

Mack keeps on going, the bend in the path is never-ending, a sure metaphor for his life right now.

The footballer's yells attack Mack's periphery. He sneaks a look back while jogging until the footballer, mid-meltdown at the ref, meets his stare. Mack forgets to watch his step and collides into another parkgoer with enough force to knock them sideways. After Mack helps her up, he keeps on jogging.

But Carly, energetic and dressed head to toe in yoga gear to top it off, doesn't do quick half-assed interactions.

'Someone's in a mood. This is a public space you know!' shouts Carly after Mack, sprinting up to him. The pair of them racing competitively, side by side.

With a hard push and a shove, she lightly states, 'I'm Carly, by the way.'

'Mack. Look, someone just stole my bike,' Mack, as he picks up the pace, 'so I ain't got time today.'

'Cute,' responds Carly, 'but how about a brand new bike, before you even leave those gates?'

That line gets Mack's attention. He stops, momentarily, only to watch Carly's smile lead to nothing, but her taking a selfie of them both.

Still, Mack cannot help but ask, 'a new bike. For real?'

'For real. I can help you redeem multiple free rewards, including red fixed gears. Just a few details to complete your sign up!' beams Carly, stretching.

Mack hits her with a roll of the eyes. 'Sign up?'

'It's super easy and now I've got your name and photo, you're halfway to completing your profile!'

Carly effortlessly dodges Mack's attempt to swipe her phone away.

After switching her angle, Carly strikes again by taking another round of photos. Mack can't avoid it.

Carly, chuckling as she flicks through the photos. 'I see you're in a hurry. I guess you could pay five credits to cover the cancellation fee and I'll leave you to it. No biggie!'

Another eye roll from Mack. 'Out of my way, man.'

Carly grabs Mack's arm and holds him firmly in place. 'I'm afraid I can't, this deal won't wait.'

Feeling trapped, Mack searches for a way out then glances at his watch for a credit count, as well as the time. Aware he's running late, he remains level-headed, polite, even. He waits for Carly to extend her arm, then swipes his watch onto hers, for the resulting transaction.

'Don't approach me again,' spits Mack, with contempt.

Mack regains his momentum. As if his mind went on tour and his body on autopilot, he's now at the edge of the long path and exhales deep once he reaches the top of the hill. If the ordeal of the Nature District is a sign of anything to come, then to be optimistic is to be a fool. He should know better.

Still, the glorious view ahead looks promising. Contemplative, Mack pulls on his vape, taking in the vast, never-ending cityscape infamously known as the Business District. Blinking signs and skyscrapers.

'Good luck today. Rooting for ya!' Carly's voice startles Mack, coming from nowhere else but inside his watch.

'Disable sharing. Letting her mess with me like that.'

'You know it ain't free,' spurts the voice of his watch, which is an algorithmic blend of Pac and Biggie. Mack's companion, assigned to him, whom he chooses to ignore. He would take it off, but it's not much good being locked out of his own home.

Nervous, Mack brushes a hand over the smooth Astroturf. He wonders if he can really switch sides. A look back at everything he's ever known reminds him that he has nothing to lose. Is this his calling, a place to belong, or just another false promise?

He has to see this one through. It's not about the money, but the slim chance that a better life could be waiting just around the corner, and he's waited long enough. There's only so much of it he can take. Those nosy neighbours, the unbearable shop doors, and last of all, those scheming little bike thieves. He's above all of that.

Stunting is to let fate decide, and Mack refuses to spend a lifetime telling himself the biggest lie, that he's a nobody. A story he's all too familiar with, from the likes of his uncle, D.

Straight after Mack passes the swift toll check to leave the comfort of Nature's wide gates, he's almost instantly overwhelmed by the unfamiliar Business District roads, and soon starts to panic. Two turns in, and he's already lost. Anything can happen here, so he's not about to waste any credits on GPS, but every street sign has long been replaced by brand logos, designer bag visuals, and the newest tech. Each eery road is identical, and completely empty.

'Chuck us a flame, pal!' A voice from across the street.

Alarmed, Mack scans this wide street, deserted except for a few parked cars. He searches the depths of his rucksack, crossing the road to meet this figure.

Dressed in all white-collar attire, this stranger greets Mack with an eager nod. 'You all right, mate?'

Mack studies this man, careful as he hands over his lighter, a black and gold memento from the old rave days, from a time before The Down Under was abolished. His lighter, and mainly the fluid that comes out of it, is a symbol of that past, when cars actually ran on diesel. Mack's favourite smell of all.

Speaking of, those few thoughts trigger memory lane to the point that, when this man lights himself a cigarette, Mack can't be sure if he's dreaming or not, when he spots it. An actual cigarette, from a classic blue and white pack. The stranger lights his and extends one to Mack, who accepts it, bemused.

Mack sparks his. 'You're smoking a cig, no vape?'

'Can't stand those things mate, I get these imported. Black market. Only sell them in Italy these days.'

Imports? Italy? Oozing business lingo and style, eyes darting from road to road, these are signs of a man who's clearly busy, reminding Mack that he also should be.

Common ground, but all Mack needs is a few directions.

'Nice one, I'm Pete.' Taking tokes, and texting.

Mack loosens up for a second, whilst savouring a smoke. 'Honestly haven't seen one of these in years, it feels good.' Mack watches the haze of smoke fly.

Pete smirks with pride. 'Not from round here? Got used to it myself, haven't seen a tree in years.'

Mack casually attempts to weave his urgent needs into the conversation. 'Got myself an interview in the centre. You know the way, Pete?'

Pete takes a long drag. 'Yeah, mate. Not far. You basically want to take a left at the end of this junction, walk straight for two minutes, a quick left and a sharp right at the data market. Then, boom.'

After blowing some smoke in Mack's face, Pete wafts it away. 'But wouldn't go there if I were you.'

Mack takes a moment, shaping up to ask, 'why?'

Pete, shifting in tone, gets to it. 'Well. You do know you can make more money in your own home, from trading? Become your own boss today, fella.'

So, it begins. Mack looks disheartened. 'I thought we were actually getting along. Don't do this.'

'We are, mate. I like you. That's why I'm offering you a proper exclusive deal, right here, right now. Today.'

Pete reveals a key from his pocket. 'See this? So much more than a key. The key to success, take it.'

Mack dashes the key, along with the last cigarette he'll ever find, and stands, defiant. 'You can't fool me, man. I don't want no pyramid scheme bullshit. I need something, like, something that's real.'

'Then take it with you Mack. Manifest it.' Pete, determined. He reveals another key from his pocket.

Once again, Mack's left searching for an escape route. That's when he spots the unthinkable.

Right across the wide road, he spots another man, walking and talking into thin air.

It's another Pete.

'What the fuck, is that you? Right there, that's literally you?' Mack, sure of himself, pointing afar.

Pete follows Mack's gaze, to see there's no one in sight. The second Pete is gone.

Another one-eighty degree swivel from Pete. 'I guess you could skip this chat, for a fee. But you will miss a once in a lifetime opportunity. Start trading today. Take advantage of the economy. Invest now. Do it.'

Mack, rubbing his eyes. 'How much this time, then? Because I'm not selling you my fucking soul.'

Eyes wide at the extortionate fare of ten credits, Mack slaps his wrist onto Pete's for a reluctant exchange, knowing to follow the protocol in fear of any consequences. Still, he barges past Pete to show him who's boss, and just like that, he's back on track, this time even more broke, and even more resentful.

'You don't know what you've cost me.'

A few strides later, Mack can't help but scour the view for the second Pete, or even the first. Both have seemingly vanished. Mack squeezes the last of his water into his hand to splash his face, twice over. Has he gone mad?

Nonetheless, the one thing Mack did gain from Pete's impromptu pitch, were the street directions. Rushing through the city streets, all of the same mould, Mack whispers Pete's instructions to himself. An act of rehearsal to keep his mind from going blank, and avoid the thought of his credit count, diminishing by the second. Relief arrives in the form of the loud, whirring data market, which reassures Mack that he's taken the right turning towards his destination. The market's closed but from the outside, each of the countless offers are available. Data, in the form of people. Mack, unsurprised, wonders if he's one of them. A sign of how life works on this side of town, with the likes of Carly and Pete, seemingly able to shop for crucial information.

It's the cost of existence these days. Every transaction, every shop door, even at schools, all activity is marked by the simple swipe of a watch. Mack remembers when they became a compulsory item, the best alternative to public outcry after the plan to implant DNA chips in your brain. D took Mack to the riots and despite his apathetic stance at the time, he's grateful to have witnessed to the last stand. Ever since then, the regime has long been silent, and of all things, that's what scares him most.

The sight of this city speaks louder than words, it's staring him in the face right now, in the form of Ad National. That logo, it's everywhere, plastered all over the data market, and lying deep within the small print of any product Mack's ever purchased, it's even stamped inside every green sandwich filling. This has been the norm for a while, the initial date is difficult to trace. First, the UK Parliament chose to outsource their media strategy and PR campaigns, with each announcement sponsored by Ad National. Then, on one ordinary Tuesday, they went and sold the whole damn thing. Transport, workforces, education, and now it seems, life itself. All brought to you by Ad National.

Back when Uncle D was around, he did warn Mack. Eat where you shit, shit where you eat, he'd say. Perhaps the first to ever flip such a known term, but D insisted it was within reason. Own. Your. Shit. He would always say it. By the age of fifteen, Mack would actually chat back and urge him to save his speech, at least until after he's finished eating. The debates, it became their daily dinnertime dynamic.

Then Mack started to rebel. Staying out late, staying up even later, unaware it would shape a huge cornerstone of his personality from thereon. Being a rebel, set against anything and everything, put Mack through half of the obstacles he's seen in his life. The other half was plain luck. D did tell him, that if he always remained silent and repressed that rebel deep down inside, he surely would not be here today. The others listened, then the others vanished. Dead or in jail it seems, including Uncle D.

The centre of the Business District looks exactly how Mack had always pictured it to look like. Unfathomably big skyscrapers, plus the small Shard, and a consistently bland non-colour scheme of black, white, and grey. Even navy seems to be a crime here. Amongst the dead sea of concrete Tetris style blocks and slick steel structures aligning each rigid pathway, one building sticks out. The only one to flash a bit of red, of course, lines the entire centre.

Ad National. Each letter, bold enough to be seen for miles. But throughout today, Mack was blinded with optimism and for that, he kicks himself, hard.

'Made it, cuz.' Mack's watch, condescending.

Why didn't he question it, where he was headed? Back against the wall, that red supermarket brick now replaced by gunmetal, Mack asks himself the exact same question a hundred times over. Each answer leads to one simple fact. Yes, there were choices, but in the end, survival takes the wheel, every single time.

He simply couldn't afford to live anymore. Days, weeks, months, years spent sitting in a small box flat, subconsciously gearing himself up to await any kind of calling, to get up, then leave without enquiring. Ever so used to that same strip of Commercial Road, all he could afford to explore since he spent most of his credits paying some guy who threatened to kill D in prison, back in 2025.

That was after hearing D cry down the phone for the fifth, or fiftieth time. Mack cannot remember. Those years a haze that truly felt like a lifetime, depression felt like a default setting, and Mack never said it to himself explicitly, but he always knew he was desperate for any way out of it. No matter how difficult, he just needed a change. So, he did it, went for it, pursued it, whatever it is, now he's walking behind enemy lines, into Ad National.

D would be screaming now, if he even cared. Mack can hardly remember his voice. Still, Mack misses D. The one man who stood by him when everyone else left. After his mum OD'd and his dad shot at her dealer, only to then get whacked himself.

'I got you D,' those few words, reassuring Mack's hesitant steps in. Rucksack on, ready. 'Let's get it.'

The twin, towering pair of indestructible doors are both firmly locked. Mack tries them again, his frustration rising. Afraid he's late, he eyes his watch:

twelve PM, on the dot. He refrains from imploding at a beeping reminder of his credit count, or lack thereof: zero credits.

Then comes an idea. As much as he hates it, this feels like a setup. From that initial call to the first few moments spent in the Business District. Mack shakes off the thought to put this information to practical use. He reaches for his back pocket, and there it is. A key. Pete's gold key, definitely not the first, nor could it be second, offered up by Pete. He must have slipped it into Mack's pocket when he stormed off. That slimy little prick.

Mack shoves the gold key into the lock, slowly twisting it. Not an inch of surprise in his expression when the door takes the key. Mack even laughs at it, the audacity. As if he's arrived at some alternate reality where Doctor Evil does actually exist, and designed this ridiculous lair himself. That would be groovy. Mack breathes in, fixes his posture, and walks on inside, to finally meet with the enemy.

'Anyone in?' Mack's voice echoes throughout the vast, empty hall, as he timidly assesses the place.

The high ceilings and floor plan of continuous rows resembling pews make it seem like a church, except here the divine ruler is capitalism. There is nothing grand, nor noteworthy, inside here, at least for Mack. Any activity is limited to blinking adverts, flashing logos, and brands that dominate from wall to wall and ceiling to floor. So loud, it feels quiet.

Mack shields himself from an imposing airline advert, where a projected plane takes flight, masking his curiosity as to what that feeling might be like.

Glass and white marble are scattered, completing the final layer of a decadent shell that must have once been a bustling epicentre for international commerce. It would have been, before Ad National initiated their plan to invest, then ultimately, buy out London. By now, the occupants are long gone.

No receptionist, HR, or PR employees to greet their guests, and Mack questions their absence. If anyone were inside, it would be easy to hold them, or some team, accountable. Instead, here he stands alone, wondering why he was ever even invited.

Alone, isolated. Until a tiny arrow flashes green.

Anxiety rises the more Mack scales the long corridor into what seems to be a waiting room, just without any budding competitors, or anyone at all. That's when the nerves begin to hit.

The bold waiting room differs in style. Whereas the office entrance offered an imposing display of harsh stone and glass, the beanbags and magazines here offer comfort, or at least try to. When Mack sits on a red beanbag, one matching his hoodie, he blends right in. He strips off the layer to look more presentable, sweaty palms whilst tapping his feet at an impossible rate, as each positive thought is hit with critical life-ending scenarios, by the second. That initial promise to himself, to show up for once and see this through, it may even get him killed.

The minutes drag, and each of Mack's actions are so repetitive, it forms a hellish loop until he looks up from his fingernails to see that the ice has all of a sudden been broken, right across from him. A table filled with an array of foods, the multitude of colours a sore sight for the eyes.

Mack ignores them, the sweets, chocolates, the biscuits. They can treat him like a kid, but he won't engage with strangers, unless he chooses to himself. It's a defensive move, to make it known, he surely isn't a pushover. Head forward, Mack eyes the wall.

'Once you pop, the fun don't stop!' shouts a crisp.

That supermarket shit all over again. This time, each of the snacks and their personalised slogans clash. The funniest part is, this is Mack's dream spread. Each specific brand, edition, flavour, all of it. The wonders of the algorithm. It's how Ad National made its name. Facilitating coded adverts to know people, better than they know themselves.

It was suggestive at first, you could even skip them. Fast forward to now, and it's a way of life, where there's nothing left to take. The end product is rather pathetic, Mack thinks to himself as a flood of nostalgic catchphrases, smart alliterative lines, and persuasive techniques counteract each other.

First the chocolate section overwhelms, then the soft drinks, then everything. Until Mack snaps back.

'STOP.'

Just like that, a wide set of doors flash green to invite Mack inside. He snorts at the thought that such a gesture could even begin to impress him. Everything in this building must have been designed by the genius of irony, or perhaps they're just too stupid to catch their own punchlines.

Classic heart thumps as Mack heads for the door, it's not like he's had to answer to anyone in years.

A sudden wave of optimism attempts to rush through his veins, but Mack shrugs it off with all of his might. He really needs to quit being so naive. Still, no controlling the mind in such situations, as all the thoughts begin to race, surge, and backflip simultaneously. He speeds up to battle his internal monologue, and ground himself in this moment.

Mack shuts his eyes, then listens to his heartbeat, and awakens. He must look like a madman to them. It's probably what they want, Mack thinks as he fixes his tie at the door, now willing to embrace his fate.

Any plan, preparation, or half-hearted attempt at self-belief heads for the door as soon as Mack steps inside it. His expression shatters to view the seat in front of him, more so an electric chair than a throne.

'Hello again, Mack. Thank you for making it on time to the interview.'

The announcement invades every claustrophobic corner in sight when Mack studies this box that would make his studio flat resemble a mansion. He cannot tell whether that soothing voice is amplified to intimidate, or actually accommodate his arrival.

'We're waiting for you. So, shall we?'

The voice of Sam, of familiarity, purely by design.

Mack's far too occupied by the devastating sight of the tech device, mounted onto this small seat. He's yet to try one, he's gone out of his way not to.

Then and there, Mack goes through it all. All the motions, every emotion. Eventually, he takes a seat, mind against it, but the body gives in. He extends a hand to grab the very device he despises to the core. The headset.

Glimpsing a bright light inside as he applies the bug-eyed goggles, Mack sinks into his seat, now committing to leave his own world, for one anew.

Expectations are one thing, yet when faced with this dull reality, as Mack forever affirms to himself, they are the root of pure delusion. Except, this isn't reality. In fact, this new environment, admittedly a close match, but it just falls short. Despite the sum of its parts, the end product is simply way too clean. He reminds himself of this, clinging onto the glass surface to the long table inside this blank canvas of a boardroom, lined with a row of identical chairs. Mack faces a translucent window at the far end of it, and descends into another compulsive round of feet tapping, then breathes out, slow, and any prior expectations set forth for this day leave with it.

In timely fashion, another surprise arrives at the door, and enters inside. An extremely familiar face, wearing his signature smirk. The one and only Pete.

'This some kind of joke?' Spine shivers shoot Mack upwards from his seat, and into the room, before Pete gestures for him to remained seated.

'Mack, it's Sam. It's a pleasure to meet with you.'

Just as Mack moves to respond, Sam reads him. 'As I did mention to you before, you would not see me, technically, as this Pete is a mere system vessel.'

Awkwardness overwhelms and Mack slowly sits himself down. 'This is just. I need the truth, man.'

With one perfectly synchronised move, Sam roams to the head of the table. His grin shifts into a sharp poker face, followed by an even wider smile.

'Countless units of this model are dotted around our London Business District. A human face, cheeky, talkative, relatable enough to maximise connections with our customers. A friend in need, that's what we do. Does that answer satisfy your query, Mack?'

Fed up of waiting, Mack refuses to be calmed or reassured, then once again, reasserts himself.

'Thought I was here for an actual interview,' avoiding Sam and each LED swirling across the wall like a desktop screensaver, 'you know, marketing, not some deal with the devil? Guess I was always right to assume, they're just one and the same.'

Sam examines Mack all too easily, which irritates him, but at least shortcuts the process. 'Of course, I'll explain. We are Ad National, an international firm who, to put it shortly, licence and operate sales across the globe to assist with your everyday life. And today, we have a proposal for you, Mack.'

'And how many questions have you asked me? Some interview.' Mack, shifting in his fabricated, virtual seat, is once again met with a brick wall.

'We understand your confusion, but this is our scheduled interview. We thank you once again. Thanks for coming.' Sam, resolute with a wide grin.

'Just get to the fucking point.' Mack, agitated.

The door, or whatever ensemble of virtual atoms that may be, swings open again. It draws to a swift close, but just before it does, a silhouette almost instantly materialises inside. As if it were Star Trek, or perhaps for Mack, a cruel dose of psychedelics.

Mack recognises that stride. With its back turned the ominous figure locks the door, using a key.

'Just get to the fucking point. Archived at twelve-fifteen PM,' it says.

It, being a person, and that person takes the seat directly opposite Mack. He shows a slim smile, and that smile, is no other than the forced grin Mack knows all too well. Only because he does it himself.

Now, looking across to this man, a carbon copy of not just his mannerisms, but an exact replica covering each minute detail. Identical, minus the human flaws. A neat trim, plus a set of pearly whites behind that smirk. Mack's world collapses around him as it all truly sinks in. He's surely met his maker.

Sam breaks the silence after this peculiar greeting. 'This is it, the purpose we brought you here for today. We present 405, our prototype to the I-Mack!'

This matter of escalation doesn't exactly warrant the same reaction from Mack. No time to process it, now the aim is to move forward. He came in today with nothing to lose, and all of it to gain. The priority in this moment is to make sure he leaves with the only two things he's got. Sanity, and the individual self. Not ten other Macks since he can barely afford to exist as just the one. The problem is an uphill struggle, a true test to keep composure, staring down a second version of himself in the eyes.

'So good to finally meet you, bro! I'll explain, but try not to panic. It's not good for your heart rate,' chimes in the alternate Mack, also known as 405.

405 reaches out to spud Mack, who slaps it away.

'See. You're the perfect candidate. Both your exceptional ability to resist manipulation and stand your ground, plus your undeniable, truly authentic individualism. Edgy, but not too urban. That's what we need!' 405, practically salivating as he pitches Mack to himself, before leaning in to the table, then shifting in tone to one of seriousness. 'A new future, and you are the key.'

Mack also leans over the table, as his forced aura of calmness slips into an edgy laugh of disbelief.

405 replicates the laugh. 'You and me, together. A new and inclusive approach, as our data tells us, minority customers are far more likely to listen to their ethnic peers. Doesn't that just sound fantastic?'

With a long chair swivel towards Sam, who's now at the head of the table, Mack allows his laugh to travel along and then come to a sudden standstill. He's more fascinated to spot a fast, uncharacteristic flash of embarrassment in Sam's eyes, which arms him with the fuel to berate Ad National even more.

That is, until 405 slams the table with force. The action draws Mack's attention back towards the man opposite, and pulls him back into this stark reality.

'It's the realness we want, G,' states 405, a chip on his shoulder. In the physical sense too, it seems.

Sam clears his throat to explain. 'He's far from finished, Mack. We do, of course, require the host's signature to continue, as we move on towards our impending U-Phone launch. Time is a factor here.'

'Funny,' says Mack, blunt as he feels himself gaining an advantage here. A short edge over his negotiators, is his ability to adjust his approach, an inherent part of being the only human in the room.

'To think anyone from round here would actually employ someone like me, you know, to make calls, hold meetings, act like I give a shit, and finally, earn just enough to survive.'

Both AIs in the room nod, in sync, their picturesque smiles summoned at will, which triggers Mack.

Mack, fed up, speaks straight from the heart. 'You really think I'd work with you lot? The sole reason life itself, in every single way, is now a dying breed?'

Mack, wiping his mouth halfway to speak the truth. 'Ad National. Because of you, I spent my entire life bored, broke, depressed, confined to the same row of streets for as long as I can remember. Other's might buy into it, but not me. I never will.'

Between that speech, a thought intrudes Mack, of himself, locked in a room, strapped to a machine. Fear is far from the outcome of this revelation, that his chances at survival are slim. To celebrate this, the chance to finally say his piece, is enough for him. But even the victories are short lived here, especially so, when one is set against themselves.

'It is funny, Mack. Funny, because I know you. Enough to know that deep down, you're relieved by this, aren't you?' 405, knowing when to counter.

That one did hurt. Mack comforts himself with a look to the floor, drowning in defeat for a moment.

This time, 405 slams the table even harder, nearly shattering the glass, if not with his hands, then with his laugh. 'Aren't you? Now we're offering you an easy way out, you can't quite believe it,' 405 towers above him, 'that you don't even have to do a thing.'

Crucial points are conceded when Mack fails to muster a reply and looks across to 405, who's now assessing himself, and joins him in the endeavour. His athletic, muscular physique, his straight posture.

405 winks at Mack, proud. 'This skin, the best of both worlds. An easy way to reach the extra nought-point-two percent of minority customers we ought to catch. Especially the females, right brother?'

That initial wink from 405 shifts to a devilish grin. 'That's all you are. You're not special, this isn't about you, and that's what hurts most. Isn't it?'

Another table slam from 405. 'But here, you can be anything, have anything. Now that's some real shit.'

Just like that, the room around them shape shifts, the LED walls twitching, time and time again. Mack's life plays out in front of them all, his dream future, informed by every algorithmic piece of data collected since the turn of the century. No more struggling, striving, instead he's at the ocean, diving.

Thereafter, footage of a slow, carefree stroll reveals Mack, holding hands with two others. His own wife, his own kid, his own family. At the end of the windy beachfront path leading to his elaborate home, stands Uncle D, ready to greet them with a smile. That's when Ad National makes their mistake.

405 shrugs off a concerned look from Sam. 'That's right. Even him, your big man Uncle D, is waiting for you here. Not out there, no one's still out there.'

His excitement reminds Mack, that it is not only himself, who benefits from making any kind of deal.

'Uncle D. He's not alive, but he's not dead, is he?' Mack, solemn, as he recalls the day that D left, or rather when he was taken. That one blurry night after the riots. That memory, not foggy enough to forget the Ad National logo spread across each police uniform, as if it were a football shirt sponsor.

405's clap pierces the air, and clears his throat. 'I've got my own Uncle D, you know. Shame you haven't anymore. Because it's true, isn't it, that without D, there's no Mack. No real fighting spirit. Just a shell of what you once were, a failed rebel. That's why we took him, and as to where he's at now, well, man, I hate to break the news to you.'

For a first, they're face to face. Mack versus Mack. The both of them, unflinching and unwilling to let slip their fixed, near identical, glares at one another.

'D did go to prison, but not the way you know it. We've got him. Suspended in time, suspended in the mind. That is, I bet you guessed it, until you sign.'

Mack follows 405's finger over to a wall, and there he is, Uncle D. Trapped, and frozen within an endless void. Predictable, thinks Mack. Still, it hurts.

'Can join him if you want, sit there brainless together. Do your ting. Or you can set him free, enjoy that dream future of yours, in this life here. All you have to do is hand over the keys, Mack.'

The keys. Ad National, for all its incredible hard work, amassing an unbreakable empire from the building blocks of self-doubt, impulsive needs, and protein shakes, all comes down to one basic core theme. Except for Mack, there is no other individual within this building, perhaps even within this entire city. Yet, still, a consumerist kingdom must quantify its wealth in the form of sales, the sale of materials.

That's what Mack's staring down at right now, which also happens to be the reason he made it into these offices today. A physical action, one that was enabled by a material possession, provided to him. Pete's gold key, Mack eyes it, lodged inside 405's pocket. Not virtual, but real. The key to making it out, and 405 is the person who reminded him of it.

'The more I look at you, I mean, really look at you,' says Mack, inviting 405 closer in towards him. 'I think to myself, if this guy's working for me out there, while I get to enjoy myself in here, the way I fucking deserve to, then why not? What's the difference if everything out there's fake, anyway?'

Sam, eagerly watching this unfold from the end of the table. As the autonomous, self-functioning administrative system, he's the closest to being a somebody in this company, which is run by nobody.

Pride consumes Sam, the more his own work bonds with its target.

Mack and 405 now reflect each other enough for Sam to finally declare it. 'Decision time?'

'If we're really doing this,' says Mack, much to the enjoyment of his counterparts, 'we'll do it my way. So, let's shake on it.'

405 glances back at Sam, his face painted with joy, as a shepherd's dog would do to his owner for finally herding in a prized sheep. He leans in further to offer Mack a firm hand. 'Exactly, bro. You said it. You chill, and I grind. You've got yourself a deal.'

This is a game to them, and Mack's well accustomed to facing bots. When programmed to crush the opponent without consequences, there is minimal room to work with. But unlike those kids in the park earlier on today, Mack has racked up enough hours, days, and years of screen time on first person shooters, RPGs, and arcade classics, to know the playing field. The crucial fact is, he was part of the era that thrived before this, that skilled crop of gamers and coders alike, those who taught these bots everything they know. Looking over to Sam and 405 right now, he finds power in the truth that, under their prosthetic skin, they are one and the same. Machine learners, which makes him their teacher.

If any of his past experiences have taught Mack anything, then the way to win this game is to dumb yourself down, conceal your cards, and know when to pounce. That way, the bots are also forced to level the playing field, to complete their primary function, which is to prolong the gaming experience and maximise engagement, to increase their earnings.

Mack's pulled this one off before, and luckily, he's up to the challenge. It's like stealing candy from a kid, or rather, headphones from a supermarket.

That explains why Mack opts for the one thing they are yet to know about him, the only weapon left in his armoury, the one he kept for himself and himself only. He closes his eyes, it's time to pounce.

'Ten. Nine. Eight. Seven. Six,' Mack counts down.

Then slowly reaches for 405's extended hand, 'wait, just a second, I want to make the terms clear again. Just to check.'

Mack opens his eyes to spot 405, clueless, and therefore powerless, knowing full well, he is unable to complete a deal without securing Mack's consent. 'If I shake, I'm selling you guys my identity. A quick yes, or no?'

Impatient nods from the AI's who, just minutes ago, were so assured. Mack continues to count. 'Five.'

Mack shrugs, nonchalant. 'Man, to think you guys should have just killed me instead.'

Although, with both eyes shut as he counts from ten, Mack fails to spot a quick, split second glance from 405 back over to Sam, before they swivel back to complete the handshake. Mack and 405 lock hands and that is when he decides on his final act, his secret weapon of meditation serving as a decoy.

'Four. Three.' Long, deep exaggerated breaths between each meditative second, said by Mack.

'Two. And, wait for it,' Mack, slowly rising, 'one!'

Mack uses the handshake to yank 405 by the hand, knock him off-balance, and swipe the gold key from 405's pocket.

The move marks the culmination of everything Mack has learned up until today. The likes of his favourite screen heroes, such as Indiana Jones, complimented with a touch of Marty McFly, as he rushes right past 405 to reach the door at the far end of the room. Even Sam is left paralysed by the move.

Mack shrugs off the pressure of this situation, away with the high stakes, to pool together all of his focus towards jabbing 405's key inside the door at the end of the boardroom. The only known way out. He also refuses to enjoy the satisfactory moment that comes when twisting the key in perfectly, for the lock to click and receive it. Access granted.

Mack entered this meeting by fighting away the positive thoughts, and must leave it that same way, if he is to ever make it out again, alive. The escape from this realm to the next is surely the hardest part, but he must maintain the momentum he's gained. No time to question why Sam hasn't moved an inch, perhaps Mack's just that good at defeating the system. 405 lays a hand on him, but he's too late.

After a strong kick of his virtual boot, straight into the virtual door, plus a fast dodge away from 405, the path to freedom presents itself. Now stood between worlds, Mack's final task is to try and battle his alternate self, before he can leave the world where anything is possible, to step back into his life, where nothing is truly possible. He's fine with that outcome. It's home after all, and that home is his.

Fake it, and you'll never make it. Just another one of Uncle D's old cliché remixes, and out of a long list, that one resonated with Mack the most. D was never a philosopher, but Mack would always stay up at night, trying to decode what he really meant by his advice. To succumb to the pressures, whether it be validation, recognition, or worse, imitation, is the only transaction that will lead you to eternal debt. Forgiving yourself for diluting yourself, bending for the rewards until there's nothing left to bend, it lays the foundation for a lonely road, to a life full of regret. That's the conclusion Mack has now reached.

In this very moment, facing the boardroom door and stuck between two worlds, Mack thinks of the ultimate lesson learned, from each debate with D, a life spent hustling, plus the harshest lesson in the form of today. That is, the only enemy worthy of his hatred is the thought of a future spent being the very person he purposefully tried not to become.

Every ounce of energy received by that overarching thought is transferred into the form of one physical action. A glorious hook to the face of 405. Mack's fist connects with 405 and knocks him down. His clone, a manifestation of everything he's not, and everything he strives to erase, is out cold.

Triumphant steps are taken by Mack to escape. What he did neglect, is that he may have spoken too soon, even revealed his cards too early, and it is not fear, but shock, that overcomes him as he steps into the room at the other end of the boardroom door. That shock is followed by frustration, and Mack feels the colour leaving his face, when stepping through the door to see, that this room is exactly the same.

Mack slams the door behind him, but not one of the occupants inside turn to acknowledge him and his grand entrance. It's as if he's invisible to them. The most terrifying part is, he's not just stumbling upon a new game to complete. In fact, it's an exact duplicate. Starting from scratch, a level to replay.

Stood in the centre of the room is 405, Sam to his left. They're concentrated on the long, exhaustive words of a third person inside the room. Those words soon become clear, taking the form of a countdown.

'Ten. Nine. Eight. Seven. Six. wait, just a second, I want to make the terms clear again. Just to check. 'If I shake, I'm selling you guys my identity. A quick yes, or no?' Each word hits and haunts Mack, as he screams in protest, watching his past, arrogant self.

'Five. Man, to think you guys should have just killed me instead.'

This unfolding comes to a sudden stop. It's as if someone has just paused a replay of one of Mack's beloved sitcoms, to rewind and play it all over again.

'You guys should have just killed me instead.'

'You guys should have just killed me instead.' Louder this time.

Those fatal words loop, over, and over, again. 'You guys should have just killed me instead.'

Each replay demands a louder yell from Mack, towards his past self, who's stood smug with pride.

When he's finally done screaming and shouting, Mack drags himself to a seat, his head hung low. It's only after another ten, or maybe a hundred, replays loop, does he notice something, as clear as day.

That glance between Sam and 405, when his eyes were firmly shut. Mack stands in front of himself, the man he was mere moments ago, enacting his master plan. That's when realises why, deep down, why he was never destined to make it out of here.

At once, both of the Mack's in the room collapse.

Then, they merge. Mack, alongside his virtual self within this second room. Thereafter, the infinite versions of Mack, all converge and collide into one.

Mack awakens, the original one. He's back in that chair, strapped to it like glue, staring into goggles, until they are lifted. He waits for his sight eyes to adjust, as if he's just come straight out of a coma.

'Signatures are all we have left, Mack. It's pure chaos without them. And with that handshake, a verbal oath, you have made yours.' Sam, above him.

Mack, shrieking to the core, finally attempts to speak up for himself, he realises he can't, now that he's robbed of perhaps the most valuable asset known to man. His voice.

'We look forward to working with you, Mack.'

405 slides into view, and rubs a hand through Mack's hair. 'Trust me, bro, I'm gassed. Rest easy.'

Just like that, Sam raises his hand, so high into the air that Mack is unable to view it any longer, then shows a polite grin as he suspends it in the air.

405 barges in to grip Mack tight and pin him down then firmly covers his mouth, just in case.

Then, faster than light, Sam swings his arm down, like a pendulum. Mack's vision, along with everything else in this small room, leaves with it.

The game is rigged and Mack, a bit-part player, is now a part of it. Paralysed, he falls into a deep sleep.

'Hey, what's good? I don't normally do this, love.'

At once, both of Mack's eyes blink open to view his feet, rapidly marching towards a lone woman.

'But you do know you could save thousands of credits a year on your life insurance, by owning a U-Phone contract, if you lock one in today?'

A quick glance from this woman, followed by a fast tap of her watch before she continues on, into a supermarket, to be greeted by a flash of green.

Leaving Mack to linger at a recognisable red brick wall, and ready to lock onto his next hourly target.

Yet, when he's whacked by an auto-trolley rolling in from behind, Mack is quick to realise that he's been beaten to its owner, by another advert, in the form of a slick young man, wearing a red hoodie.

After that deal is sealed, both Mack's share a nod.

Now intending to expand his reach beyond this deserted entrance, Mack slows his pace to see it.

A young, cheeky looking teenager, bopping his head along to a pair of headphones, while he races past Mack, causing him to swivel from left to right.

The teenager rides a red fixed-gear bike, matte black handle bars. With his eyes glued to the bike, Mack pauses, to consider a thought.

There's too many of us, thinks Mack. Too many.

Motionless, Mack scans around, to see that not just one of his counterparts, but five others, have also noticed it, and thought something of the same.

Together, they count down from ten…

About The Author

Raphael Agbowu D'Cruz is a writer from Peckham.

With roots in Britain, India, and Nigeria, Raphael studied history at the University of Manchester, to explore the contexts behind his global origin story.

There, his interests were found more in the effects of great historical events upon people, over politics. This led Raphael to writing as a form of expression.

Following a master's degree in screenwriting, the craft of storytelling became an outlet for Raphael's culturally focused perspective. Whether on the page or screen, he writes to present thought-provoking social commentaries, backed by original concepts.

Commercial Road is Raphael's first ever book. He is also creating a series of films, titled *Lost and Found*.

Printed in Great Britain
by Amazon